BLACKER THAN BLACK OPS

by

Deryk Cameron Stronach

Acknowledgements

Thanks to Mrs Sreenivasan Jayandi (Mrs Pathy), Mr Sheik Alaudin Mohd Ismail for their invaluable criticism and comments.

Thank you to the Internet for allowing me to keep in daily contact with my family in Singapore, Mary and Monica, stay safe.

George Baey, Hang in there mate. You are a fighter.

Special thanks to all Health Care Workers and front-line staff worldwide for all the work you have done in these troubled times.

All royalties from this book will be given to a charity for Health Care Workers.

Blacker Than Black Ops

Contents

Prelude

There is the written word in folklore books, and there is reality. The problem is that the folklore is real, but nobody is allowed to know.

Col. Hamish Hamilton had been settling into his forced retirement in the generally quiet seaside town of Largs, Scotland when he was dragged back into active service in Military Intelligence. Hamilton is a boundary walker, one who has the gift of second sight. It was this gift General Maxwell believed, needed to solve the unexplained kidnappings of young men and women from the nearby Isle of Cumbrae by shape-shifting aquatic folklore creatures called kelpies.

General Maxwell, a moustached gentleman of military bearing, the bearer of a nose coloured by other people's whisky, headed MIC, Military Intelligence Cryptids, had done the dragging, he had also done the retiring when he thought Hamilton had cracked up. Promoting Hamilton to a full colonel as a sweetener, he also gave him an assistant, Capt. Alison Macduff. Janet Drummond, the widow of Hamilton's friend and former MIC mentor, Jack Drummond, joined Macduff and Hamilton. Janet is a selkie from the Shetland Islands. Selkies can be human or seal by removing or replacing their seal skin. They also live extremely long lives, Janet was in her two hundred and somethingth year but looked in her twenties. A fate that many women would gladly suffer.

As the operation progressed, Hamilton was given a kitten by the Guardian, Princess, which wanted to be treated like royalty when she was awake, which was not that often it seemed. The general gave or assigned Major, an ex-military dog, a Malinois with PTSD from service in Iraq and Afghanistan as Ham's bodyguard.

Three further characters joined the team for the kelpie operation; all were SBS operators, Sgt. John Paterson, who had initially been with naval intelligence, decided at the end of the mission to remain with the team, whereas Sgt. Rob Ingram and Cpl. Jaimie Nicholls decided to return to their duties with the SBS in Poole, Dorset, down on the south coast of England.

There are more than kelpies and selkies in the waters around Scotland. Hamilton realised that his retirement would have to wait until he could train Macduff or at least help her to realise that she too was a boundary walker.

Dartmoor

It sat on a tombstone in an old forgotten graveyard attached to a long overgrown and uncared for settlement on Dartmoor and waited. Others had come and gone, but they were not the right one, not enough vitality, not enough energy. It had waited tens of years; it could wait for many more if need be, but it was getting hungry.

This dull, cold grey October afternoon showed promise though, as the kuri could feel his energy from afar. It willed him to come nearer. It yearned for him. If it could have spoken aloud, it would have called him to its lair. It had waited, it had examined, it had rejected, but this one, this one it wanted. It began to crave his energy. Nearer and nearer he came. Physically tired from the walk, but emotionally strong, determined, he was just what it wanted.

As he came to the graveyard, he took out his map and compass, and paused, just checking, not stopping, he kept on his course and replaced the items. He knew where he was going.

The kuri attached itself to the young man as he passed. He never noticed, he became a host to the parasite without feeling or even knowing of its presence. The kuri explored its new home; it delved into his emotions and memories. It had been a good choice; this was fine dining to the soul taker. It could devour the soul quickly over a few months and send the soul to Hell, or it could nibble and savour the experience over years if not decades, enjoying the gradual torment and destruction of its host. If it had lips, it would have smacked them; the second choice was far more enjoyable.

The young man had love in his heart and determination in his very being. The kuri licked its metaphorical lips again while it decided which to drain first.

The young SBS corporal marched on, thinking that the weekend on the desolate moor would strengthen his mind and body. Aware of his surroundings, Jaimie Nicholls' mind wandered to his fiancé back in Poole, waiting for him to return that night. The kuri felt his emotions and dreams; it salivated with anticipation. Soon its thirst, its hunger, its craving would be sated.

A Matter of Order

Hamish Hamilton, known to nearly everyone as Ham, was a man in his sixties. He stood with his shoulders rounded, and his face partially hidden. The part that was exposed showed his lower face covered in a neat grey-white beard dotted with beads of water from the light but cold rain. Beneath the pulled down grey fabric Kangol flat cap, a pair of intelligent eyes that had seen too much, noticed Major's reaction, a flick of the left ear, a twitch of the nostrils, then he too heard the intruder. He knew those military footsteps anywhere.

"Evening general. What drags you away from the warmth of your office?"

"Why can't you move down to Whitehall instead of hiding in the wilderness Hamilton?" Ham nodded his head slightly and stood up from where he had been leaning on the railings overlooking the stone and pebble beach with its noisy lapping waters. He turned to meet the general. A smile that was not entirely friendly crossed his face. He did not reply; the general already knew the answer. The two men studied each other for a few moments, Ham with his hands casually in the chest pockets of his olive-green Barbour jacket and the general with his twitching moustache, under his whisky red nose. Major, the Malinois, looked from one to the other, juggling his eyebrows in concentration. Although Major, an ex-special forces dog, had PTSD, Post Trauma Stress Disorder, he was given to Ham by the general as a bodyguard. In the small rucksack on Ham's back, Princess the young cat given to Ham by the Guardian, slept, something which even at her young age she was fast becoming an expert. Princes, a member of cat royalty, slept, poohed and slept, but she had saved Ham's life in the past. She was part of Ham's entourage.

"We have a situation in the Orkney Islands, on the island of Hoy to be exact." General Maxwell looked at Ham, but Ham did not react. "There has been some encounters and possibly some abductions or murders." Still no reaction from Ham, so he looked left and right as if checking that they were alone. "Nuckelavees."

Ham did react, his eyebrows raised sharply and then settled into a frown.

"That's bad. Nuckelavees are evil creatures, but what has brought them onto the land? They've stayed in the water for a hundred years."

"That my dear Colonel Hamilton is why I employ you. To sort out these little problems." The general stated flatly twisting his lips to a smirk as he said so. Hamilton had taken the bait.

"You forget again that I am semi-retired and that you retired me if I remember correctly."

"Well, get your semi-retired self, up to the Orkneys."

"Sorry, I need to go down south before I go up north." Ham flipped a finger south and then his thumb in the general direction of north.

"Yes, yes. I'm sure you have your plans, but you need to go up and sort out this Orcadian monster first before somebody kills it and puts it on show, or it kills any more people. If the public finds out that these things exist all Hell will break loose."

"Again, sorry, but I must sort out some other business first. Then I shall go and deal with the nuckelavee."

"What?" Pause for breath. "Hamish, what can be more important than dealing with the nuckelavees?"

"Sergeant Ingram, you know the chap from the SBS that we used on the kelpie problem last year, says that Corporal Nicholls, the other SBS operator we used then, is in trouble and needs my help." The general waited impatiently, didn't this man understand the priority. Was this from some strange sense of loyalty? The general could get Hamilton any SAS, SBS, SRS operator he wanted.

Ham continued, "I will need them both. I want them because they know that cryptids do exist and I don't want any more people involved than need to be. Plus, I don't think it is just about the nuckelavees."

What about Captain Macduff and Sergeant Paterson?"

"Macduff is at RAF Brize Norton on the four weeks Special Forces Parachute Course, she should finish in a couple of days, and Paterson is on a helicopter refresher course, maybe another week to go for him. You authorised the training, remember?" The general

nodded. He did not look happy. He looked thoughtful.

"How long?"

"Me? I'm driving down tomorrow. Just a few days, I think."

"Why not fly? It would be quicker. That's why I want you

down in Whitehall dammit."

"General, I will tackle the Orcadian problem, but I must sort out

this lad's problem first. I'll take the car as I think I'll need to travel

about a bit. I think I might have to visit Ambrose. Don't worry; I'll

get the team together and deal with the nuckelavees in good time.

Anyway, general, we both know the only reason you come up here is

to drink my whisky. Janet should still be at my apartment. She'd

love to meet you. God knows why. Bring your bodyguard; he'll

freeze out there. Who is out there; Gilchrist?" The general nodded,

and Ham tutted and waved out into the darkness for the bodyguard to

join them. They turned and walked back along the promenade to

Ham's apartment.

They argued like an old married couple, they both respected even liked each other, but they would never say it.

Graverobbers

"The nuckelavee, eh? Jesus! Didn't think I'd ever get involved with one of them. Nasty buggers by all accounts. I wonder what triggered it or them to come on land?" Ham mused aloud.

"Haven't got a clue, old boy." The general replied as they settled down in the living room. "Something else, but I don't know if it is related, there's been some graverobbing going on in that area."

"Graverobbing! Bloody Hell, whatever next? On Orkney?"

"And on the islands and the Scottish mainland, a real Burke and Hare[1] business. Totally out of order." Ham sipped his whisky thoughtfully. 'Why would someone want bodies in this day and age?" The general shrugged. Janet Drummond sat on the sofa beside Ham; she also looked thoughtful.

---

[1] The infamous pair, William Burke and William Hare robbed graves in Edinburgh in 1828. When they could not find enough newly buried bodies, they started to create their own.

"What do you think, Janet?" asked Ham looking at her over his glass.

"I know that all sea creatures avoid the nuckelavee. They are wild creatures with no souls, but they rarely go on land. I haven't heard of this for over a hundred years. A hundred years! Why now? Doesn't make sense, does it?"

"If you hadn't killed Maddox last year, I would suspect that he was somehow involved in this. It's got his fingerprints all over it."

"I don't think he died." Ham looked at the general, who looked shocked.

"But you reported that the speedboat he was escaping on was shot to pieces by the helicopter?"

"Yes that happened, and we saw no sign of life after the attack, but..."

"But?"

"You know that having the 'second sight', I can usually see how long a person has to live?"

"Yes." replied the general impatiently.

"Although I don't see how Maddox cannot have died last year, my second sight indicated that he would live for a while longer. I never thought about it at the time."

"Why didn't you say this in your report? I would have had people looking for him."

"My second sight has never let me down, but I saw the mess the helicopter's minigun made of the boat, totally shredded it. Should I believe my eyes or my second sight?"

A Walk by the Quay

Ham set off in the early hours arriving at the Thistle Poole Hotel, in the late afternoon. He chose the place as it was pet friendly. Major was hotel friendly, so it was a good match.

It was when he was unpacking his overnight bag that he realised that he had a stowaway. He then phoned Janet to tell her that she could stop looking for Princess as she had decided to take a holiday. He hoped that the hotel was Princess friendly.

That evening Rob Ingram joined him for a bite to eat, during which time they spoke generalities. After their meal, Ham collected the beasts who had also been fed and watered by the hotel; all four wandered off the short distance to the Quay area. It was there that Rob told how Jaimie's attitude and behaviour were going to see him RTU'd, or Returned To Unit, the ultimate punishment for any special forces operator. Rob was really worried for him.

Ham asked when and how Jaimie had changed. Rob answered as best as he could, but he was reluctant to talk about the last two missions Jaimie had been on, because of the secretive nature of their work. All he would say was that the bosses were not happy with Jaimie's performance and that he seemed to be getting worse. There is a loyalty in both directions in the service, but Rob said, Jaime was pushing the limits, and he would soon have to be 'let go'.

Ham asked a lot of probing questions, gradually pushing the time scale back to when Rob had seen the beginning of Jamie's decline. As best as Rob could work out, it was on the return of Jaimie from some solo march over Dartmoor, that it had all started.

Jaimie came back from his yomp, a Royal Marine slang term for a long-distance loaded march, into the arms of his loving fiancée Martine. Martine Saunders was a Royal Navy sub-lieutenant, who was giving up her commission for the love of her life because although an officer and an NCO, Non-Commissioned Officer, could now marry, it was still frowned upon by those above. The return of the hero had gone as expected, but uncharacteristically, Jaimie had woken up the next day in a foul mood. It was as if he was upset and looking for an argument. Initially, Martine had thought he was just tired. She knew that his work could be very tiring and stressful She gave him a bit of space for the next few days, but when his attitude continued, she temporarily and then permanently, moved out of his flat and back into the Officer's Quarters.

Martine knew Rob well, and seeking him out, asked him, what was going on. She told him that she suspected that Jaimie had met another girl when he was away on Dartmoor. Rob had noticed the change in Jaimie's behaviour but said that he did not think that that was the case. He knew how much Martine meant to him. Rob had tried to talk to Jaimie, but it had not gone well, Jaimie had pushed him away.

It had gotten gradually worse, with the lieutenant and then the captain calling Rob in for a chat about Jaimie. Jaimie had then received a summons for an informal chat, that was stilted and awkward. The captain sent Jamie to a service psychiatrist, but that also had not gone well. Jamie had only gone because it was an order to go. The psychiatrist report stated that Corporal Nicholls was angry and evasive. The captain arranged for Jamie's medical leave, during which time he sat alone in his room or drank alone in the bar. Rob knew that the options on the table were that Jaimie, would be RTU'd or medically discharged with PTSD, Post-Traumatic Stress Disorder, that was why he had called the colonel. The colonel, Rob knew, had PTSD, maybe because he understood, he could help in some way. Jaimie's career and possibly life was on the line.

Ham knew or at least suspected the truth as soon as Rob had said that Jaimie had changed on his return from Dartmoor. Ham said that he would go to Royal Marine Base Poole the next day and speak to Jaimie's CO, Commanding Officer, if he was free. Ham reassured Rob that he would sort something out. He needed a nightcap in the bar to get some warmth into his old bones, time to think things through and to make a phone call to the general.

After the whisky, which Rob offered to pay for because he had drunk so much of Ham's up in Largs, Rob left, leaving Ham to his thoughts. Ham played with his glass, twisting it around in his fingers not seeing what he was doing. When he decided what to do, he went to his room and made the call; he knew what he wanted to do. He made two phone calls, one to the general and one to RAF

Brize Norton.

RMB Poole

Ham had just finished his breakfast when Macduff entered the restaurant.

"Have you eaten?" he asked. Macduff shook her head in reply.

"It was too early when I left." Ham stood up and picked up a piece of buttered toast.

"I'm taking Major for a quick walk. You'd better get something 'down you'. We leave when I get back." He handed her the menu.

"Where are we going?"

"We have an appointment with the second in command of the SBS. Get your order in, or you're doing a takeaway." With that, he walked away. Macduff shook her head. He was always doing this to her. She looked around for the waitress

When Ham returned with Major and Princess, Macduff had finished and was sipping her second coffee. He nodded and waved for her to follow. They went to his car, where he handed her his keys.

They arrived at RMB Poole and after showing their MI5 IDs were directed to the SBS HQ, where a young officer guided them to the second in command's office, a Major Sellick. Ushered into Major Sellick's office introductions were made. The major, a bulky man with a board chest under a freckled face and sandy coloured hair, thanked the young officer who quickly departed from the room.

The major apologised that the CO could not be there, but he was away on official business and asked what he could do for them. The major also stated that his instructions were to offer to his visitors all assistance that did not affect the operations of the service. There was a glint of annoyance in his eyes; nevertheless, he asked again how he could help. Ham explained that he was there because of Cpl. Jaimie Nicholls. Major Sellick sucked in his breath, raised a finger in the wait sign, he was used to people obeying and leaned forward to his intercom, through which he asked for Major Redman and Captain Lewes to report. Sellick stated that he was aware that Corporal Nicholls was having problems, but Major Redman as his squadron commander and Lewes as his troop commander were more acquainted with the case. They must have been in the same building as they knocked and entered a short while later.

Introductions made, they gave their report and opinions, much as Rob had stated the night before. The only additional information was that Jaimie had got drunk the night before and made a fool of himself in the bar. Getting drunk was certainly not unheard of in the military, but Jaimie was getting a reputation as a bad drunk.

Ham asked for their impression on Rob Ingram. In comparison, this report was glowing. Ham thanked them, and Major Sellick dismissed them with thanks. Sellick looked at Ham and steepled his hands. Ham thought for a moment, then asked to see Nicholls, after which he would like to see Sgt. Ingram and then the major again in say, half an hour. Sellick nodded and then buzzed through asking for Sgt. Ingram to report to his office.

"I'm not going to ask what this is all about. We don't ask those type of questions here, but I'll tell you that Nicholls had been a damn good JNCO, he had a good future in the SBS until recently, and it would be a shame if he had to be kicked out, but…" Ham just nodded in understanding.

Rob reported a few minutes later, and Sellick ordered him to take the party to Jaimie.

They found Jaimie still asleep in his bed, still dressed and still a bit drunk. When roused, he blearily focused on them. Ham could see the kuri trying to hide behind Jaimie.

"Colonel, Alison, how nice to see you." The room stank of old booze and sweat. Major growled, baring his teeth, and Princess started to get upset, raising her fur and spitting. Ham gave Princess to Macduff and asked her to take Major out of the room, which she managed to do after a struggle. Rob looked horrified; he did not understand; the animals had loved Jaimie.

Ham turned to Rob and said, "I can fix him, but I think it is too late to save his career here. They won't trust him; you know that." Rob nodded. "Get him sobered up and bring him to the Major's office in good order." Rob nodded his thankful agreement. "Rob, I know you said that you wanted another year in the SBS after the kelpie business, but I would like you to reconsider and move over to MIC with Jaimie now. You can both still be officially in SBS, but I want you to keep an eye on Jaimie." Ham knew he was not playing fair. He knew that he was playing the man, but he wanted the pair of them on his team as they already knew about the cryptids and had proven themselves to be good operators. They were more than a couple of heavies, they had brains, well, normally. Ham had seen the kuri as soon as he saw Jaimie, but he had already guessed that it would be there. Jaimie would need to meet an old friend of Ham's; Ambrose. Ham looked sideways at Macduff, who saw the look and frowned back, 'what was the old goat up to now?'

A Visit to Ambrose

Ham drove the lead car with Jaime and Rob who sat in the rear seat. Macduff followed in the second car with the beasts, as they could not travel with Jaimie and his 'guest'. The weather was damp and grey, with a hint of sunshine.

Major Sellick had released Jaimie and Rob to Ham after a private discussion with his absent boss on the telephone. Jaimie had to go, whether it was by RTUing or a transfer to another department, that did not matter, especially when Ham explained that the SBS budget would not be affected by the missing SBS men. Rob had decided to accept the detachment to MIC. Both were now part of MIC, but they were still members of SBS, be it that all their costs were taken care of from a black budget.

Jaimie, sat crumpled in the corner of the rear seat, cradled by a concerned Rob. Ham watched the car following and also watching the road behind that car. He had to make sure that nobody followed them.

They drove down towards Newquay. Ham would stop every so often to make sure that the cars did not have a tag. He was sure that they were clean because he did not have 'that itch'. As he drew near Newquay, he turned off for Newquay airport. Near the airport, he turned down to Saint Mawgan which lay in the valley, quiet and secluded. Checking that Macduff was still with him, he turned off a partially hidden side road and followed the rough road into the thickening forest.

Ham braked. The stag stood in the middle of the road. The stag its head crowned by a huge set of antlers stood proud and stared the car down. Ham stopped the engine, applied the handbrake, told his passengers to remain where they were, and got out. He stood by the car and looked at the stag. The stag watched the second car arrive. It drew up behind Ham's car. Ham signalled for the other occupants to remain in the car and returned his gaze to the stag. The stag looked back at Ham until they nodded slowly at each other, then the stag, seemingly satisfied, strode off the road and bounded into the forest. Ham got back into the car. He started the engine and drove off slowly.

Driving further into the forest, it struck Ham that the forest seemed deeper than the valley should be. He knew why; this was an Enchanted Forest; it did not exist in the 'real world'.

They came to a small quaint cottage that came straight out of a Disney princess cartoon. You half expected Snow White or Sleeping Beauty to come singing out of the door. What appeared was no beauty, just an old rotund man with a long bushy white full-set beard. On the back of his head was perched a pale blue baseball cap. He wore blue jeans and a red checked shirt, partially covered with a black waistcoat. He looked like an off-season, Santa Claus.

Ham waited until the second car joined them, then he got out and signalled them to join him.

"So Hamish Hamilton, what are you after this time? I never see you unless you want something."

Good afternoon Ambrose, I have someone here who needs your help."

"Yes, I see him. Bring him in. The rest of you are welcome," said the old man with the rosy cheeks and sparkling eyes, turning and re-entering the cottage. Everyone followed.

"How long ago did the kuri attach itself to this young man?" Ambrose asked when they were all inside.

"About six months," replied Ham.

"Terrible, terrible. Poor boy. There is some three-hundred-year-old whisky in the cupboard over there, help yourself." came the voice, as the old man disappeared into another room. Ham collected the decanter and offered it to Macduff who declined and Rob who accepted eagerly. Rob had never heard of three hundred years old whisky, twelve, fifteen, eighteen, but never anything like three hundred. He sipped it and decided that it was truly the drink of the Gods.

The old man returned, stood in front of Jaimie and handed him down a rough ceramic bowl containing a thick green liquid. A meter or so away, Ham could smell the awful mixture and wrinkled his nose in disgust. He turned his face so that Jaimie would not see his reaction.

"Drink this boy. Hear me, creature, leave this boy and return to your lair. If you go to anyone in this area, I shall send you to your master in Hell. You will be no more on this earth. Boy, drink the liquid, now, all of it. Beautiful girl make sure he drinks all of it." The strange old man looked at Macduff and smiled, but the smile had a leer, a lust. Macduff didn't find it offensive, strange, but not offensive. He was just an old man.

Jaimie hesitated, the turmoil in his mind was obvious to see, but then he drank the liquid as ordered. Nothing happened for a while, everybody waited, but only Ambrose seemed unconcerned. It took a few moments, then suddenly Jaimie stood up, and his head fell back, his chest thrust out as if it would burst. Jaime gasped, he collapsed back in the chair and slept. Macduff wondered what the Hell had happened; Ham had not told her about the kuri, or their host. Rob shook his head slowly wondering if he had made the right choice. He liked working with Ham and Macduff, they seemed like good bosses, the colonel knew his business, and the captain did not shove her rank in your face, but he realised that this was going to be weird work.

There's No Place Like Home

Jaimie was still out cold, Rob sat beside him, giving him the odd glance, Macduff tried to get a signal on her phone and Ham was watching her with an amused grin, Major and Princess slept on the rug in front of the log fire, Ambrose walked in with a large plate full of sandwiches and chicken drumsticks.

"Help yourselves; I'll bring in some coffee." He returned a few moments later. "Coffee ok for everyone?" he queried

"Any chance of a tea, please Ambrose?" asked Ham. Ambrose touched the mug nearest Ham and said, "That'll be your one, then." Ham smiled. Macduff looked a little puzzled. She looked at the mug and her eyebrows creased.

"Can I have a tea as well please Mr Ambrose?" she asked.

Ambrose touched the mug nearest to her and said, "That will be yours then. Sergeant Ingram, coffee?" Rob took the proffered coffee and sipped it as he could see it was steaming hot. It was good. He sat down, wondering how Ambrose knew he was a sergeant as nobody had said. He took another sip of the fine coffee and looked at the colonel, who was doing his best to surpass a grin.

"Ambrose, how long before your potion takes effect?"

"The kuri has already gone, but his mind needs time to repair itself. He'll be right by morning. I've made up rooms for you all upstairs. Choose your room. Don't worry; he'll be safe to travel tomorrow afternoon. Do you want to stay with him or separate rooms? He'll be quite safe alone, but I shall leave the choice up to you. Don't worry; he'll be right as rain by the time he gets to Scotland." Ham nodded and drank his tea, made just the way he liked it. He smiled at Ambrose.

"Rob take Jaimie upstairs and get him into bed. Are you going to stay with him?" Rob nodded, he stood up and easily carried Jaimie upstairs.

On the stairs, he turned and asked Ambrose which room he should use.

"Any one, dear boy, take your choice." Rob went upstairs and opened the first on the right. It was a large room with two beds.

Stripping off Jaimie's shoes and outer clothing, he tucked him into bed.

Just as Rob was going down the stairs, Macduff passed him coming up. He squeezed into the corner of the bend in the stairs to let her pass. He watched her go up the second leg of the stairs and before he could stop her enter the first room on the right. Having caught sight of this, Rob was about to go up to tell her, but he realised that she would learn that it was Jaimie's room soon enough. He waited; she did not come out. Puzzled, he went back up and knocked on the door. There was no reply. He opened the door and saw Jaimie, fast asleep on the bed. Macduff was not there. He looked around, but he still could not find her. Puzzled, he left the room and looked up and down the corridor, before going downstairs. Just as he was about to turn the corner of the stairs, he looked over and saw Macduff leave the room he had just left. His jaw dropped and he stood on the half landing as she approached.

"You been standing there the whole time?" she asked as she came down and squeezed passed him. Rob looked at her and then at the door. He shook his head and went downstairs.

When he reached the bottom, he excused himself and went out the front door. Something else from his memory puzzled him. Walking a short distance, he turned and stared back at the cottage. It took a few moments for him to realise that Ham, having followed him out, stood in front of him. There was no upper floor, at all.

"Come inside Rob, and I'll introduce you to my old friend Ambrose." Rob followed Ham indoors. Ham pointed to a seat where Rob had sat earlier. Rob sat.

Ham picked up the mug of tea that he had been drinking earlier. He was not surprised to find it full and still hot.

"Ambrose, you've had your fun, do you tell them or shall I?" Ambrose chuckled, sipped his whisky and waved a finger at Ham. A splash of whisky landed on his finger. Ambrose licked it clean.

"You'd better put them out of their misery Ham. If you trust them, then so do I."

"Macduff, Rob, let me introduce you to Merlinus Ambrosius, probably better known to you as Merlin. He's lived in this Enchanted Forest for hundreds of years, ever since he was supposedly trapped under a stone by a water nymph. Very careless old chap. Rob, you remembered that when we arrived that there was no upper floor and yet Jaimie is lying in a bed upstairs. Whatever door you entered would be your room. He loves that trick, caught me out when Jack Drummond first brought me here. The coffee, tea or me trick, come on Ambrose, that was cheap. The food, a wave of his hand and a little chant and hey presto whatever food you want. Which one of you had been thinking of sandwiches and drumsticks?" Rob raised his hand slowly. "The stag, that was our shape-shifting friend here. Wanted to see who was visiting. If he didn't want you to visit, it would have stepped out the way, and you would have exited the valley none the worse for wear. Anything I missed? Ambrose is the only person I know who could have exorcised the kuri. The kuri lives in Dartmoor waiting for a suitable subject, then like a parasite, it latches onto its prey, invisible, undetected even by the host. And yet, there it is draining the emotion and soul from the person until he or she is either driven to suicide or just loses the will to live. No other person I know could get rid of it; just Merlin Ambrose." Ham pointed to Ambrose who took a slight bow in as coy a manner as he could muster, failing badly because of the big boyish grin on his face.

A small thing, be careful when he asks you what you want for breakfast tomorrow because that is what you'll get. Don't try to be funny; Ambrose has a funny sense of humour, if you ask for camel, you will get a camel, stuffed and cooked."

Return to Largs

After an uneventful breakfast, without a camel in sight, they prepared to leave.

As they drove away, Macduff looked in her rear mirror and laughed.

"He's wearing a pale blue robe with a pointed hat with a kink in the end, isn't he? His beard is longer, dangling down to his feet. Probably got an owl perched on his shoulder," stated Ham in a bored manner not bothering to look back. Ham raised his hand and waved back at the wizard who was jumping around as if dancing a jig. "He does it all the time; Merlin thinks it's funny ever since he saw the film. Maybe it was the first few times. You'll see him again in your career. Always take someone with you, he's a randy old goat, doesn't act his age." Ham's warning tone had a hint of boredom or was it indifference; you can only see the same thing so many times.

Rob and Jaimie would return to Poole in Ham's car to collect all their clothing and belongings and sign back in their issued kit. Ham told them to retain their SBS uniform and IDs as they were still technically in the SBS and may need them sometime. Weapons and other specialist equipment, he told them, would be issued later. They were to make their way up to Largs and report to him there.

Ham sat slouched down in the passenger seat of Macduff's car with the beasts asleep in the back.

"Sir, I didn't want to ask in front of everyone, but what are nuckelavees?"

"Nuckelavees are Orcadian, that's the Orkney Islands, creatures. They normally live in the depths between the islands. Last sightings before recently were a hundred plus years ago. When they do come on land, by all accounts, they cause chaos, killing people, and if they cannot kill people, they kill their livestock. Even their breath can kill.

I want you to imagine a man with a very large head, very long arms sitting on a horse. The horse has only one large red eye in the centre of its head. The man's arms are so long that they almost touch the ground, all the way down. Ok? Now, the man and horse are one creature. Next, I want you to imagine that the creature skinned, no skin, no fur or scales, just muscle, bone and pulsating arteries and veins, like in a weird living biology book. To put it politely, it is not a pretty sight.

But, what gives the nuckelavee its reputation, is that they have no soul, they attack for no reason, they don't need to eat, although they do, they don't do it for pleasure, they just do it. There is only one thing they fear and that, strangely enough, them being aquatic creatures, is water, freshwater. Cross freshwater, they cannot follow you, throw freshwater at them, and they will scream and run away in a rage.

Something and I don't know what yet, has brought them back onto land and one way or another, we have to stop them."

But that's not all is it?" Macduff asked.

"Graves, somebody is doing a bit of graverobbing."

"What? Graverobbing? Who on earth goes graverobbing in this day and age? Are they connected?" she paused in thought and drove on a while before she continued, "Do nuckelavees rob graves?"

"No, but I suspect that it is all connected, maybe too well, something smells about this. We do not see the whole picture yet. I just feel as if someone is playing a game with me, with us. The only way to find out is for us to go to the Orkney Islands. But first, to Largs. Lead on Macduff!" he misquoted from Shakespeare's Macbeth. She groaned.

"It's 'Lay on Macduff,'" she corrected.

"I know," replied Ham, "but that wouldn't make sense, would it?" he said settling into the passenger seat. "Drive on Macduff, just hasn't got the same ring about it."

She groaned again and drove off. It was going to be a long drive.

The Gathering

Ham had gone out to take Major for his evening walk. It was late, it was cold, and it was dark. Ham did not notice, he found his favourite spot out by the boating pond and leaned against the railings there, looking out over the black waters of the River Clyde. Again Major notified him of the pair arriving, this time by wagging his tail and looking in their direction. Ham could hear them clearly, but he waited until they were nearer before he stood up and turned toward them.

"All sorted?' he asked.

"If you mean Poole boss, yes. I think they were glad to get rid of us." Rob grinned, Jaimie looked at him and grinned also, but in thanks. Jaimie knew it was he that they were glad to be rid of, not Rob. Good mates stuck together.

"If you mean the accommodation, yes too. Janet gave us the keys to the house on Brisbane Road. We can see the work done on that place, and I don't mean normal civilian stuff. It's secure, tight as a drum. It's as if you knew we were coming back." Rob left that hanging in the air. Ham ignored the comment; he had been preparing the place for them since the kelpie operation the previous year, getting the place selected, purchased, 'adjusted' by specialist military contractors. Their weapons and specialist gear would be safe there when they were elsewhere on business. Even the garage was modified so that their business car with its various hidden compartments and equipment would be secure. There own cars would have to take their chances on the driveway. Largs was not a high crime area, and the chances of burglary or car theft were slim, but Ham could not take the chance of a local hoodlum getting in and accessing the operators kit.

He had overseen the work on the house between the two missions he had undertaken since the kelpie mission which had involved Rob and Jaimie. One was the negotiated truce between the fish farmers and the 'Blue Men of the Minch' near the Inner Hebrides he had conducted with Janet's help and the other the renewal of the treaty with the fairies living under Knock Hill overlooking Largs. Both were tricky as he had to negotiate without the fish farmers or the general public realising what he was doing on their behalf.

Ham briefed them on their next mission, going up to the Orkney Islands to deal with the nuckelavee. He gave them the general's assistant Ms. Lucinda Miller's telephone number and told them to arrange with her for any equipment, weapons etc. that they thought they might need. He told then to err on the side of more rather than less. He also told them to get silver dumdum bullets as part of their ammunition, not all weapons could handle silver ammunition, and not all creatures would die once shot with normal ammunition.

They had talked on the way back to Ham's flat on Fort Street; he had invited them back for a nightcap. Noticing that Jaimie was quiet and withdrawn Ham spoke to him.

"You were unlucky with the k

kuri, it probably chose you because you are strong, not just physically, but mentally. There is nothing you could have done. A weaker person would probably have committed suicide or gone crazy. Jaimie, I need you on top form. Get yourself fit, and snap out of it, ok?"

"Yes, boss," came the reply.

"Rob, once you have sorted everything out with Ms. Miller, and you have your goodies, we're off north. She's pretty damn good so the stuff will arrive pretty quickly, a day or so. We'll drive up in a couple of cars; it'll be easier to carry all the gear and the animals and to move around when we're there. Anything you need local, contact Captain Macduff or myself. Right, let's get that nightcap. I'm afraid it's not three hundred years old, but it'll have to do."

Road Trip

Two days later, after breakfast at the Green Shutters in Largs, the three cars headed north. Ham, Macduff, Janet and the two beasts in the first car, Rob and Jaimie in the second and John, who had returned the evening before in the third. All three cars left Largs on the Haylie Brae and followed the A760, to Glasgow, and from Glasgow to Stirling, and on to Perth. While the first two cars continue north, John turned off and headed towards Arbroath and RMB Condor.

The two cars continued north until they reached Thurso. From Thurso, they took the ferry to Stromness on the Mainland of the Orkney Islands. Their journey was not quite over, they had to take a further ferry to Moaness on the Orkney island of Hoy and then follow the long and winding B9047, down, along, up, down and around Hoy until they reach the remote house overlooking the sea that Ms. Miller had rented for them.

Waiting to meet them was the landlady, a startled old lady who stared at Janet. Her stare was very obvious and made Janet uncomfortable. Ham looked from one to the other wondering what was going on.

"Are you related to Janet Drummond, a grand-daughter perhaps? You are the spitting image of her." Janet stared back, momentarily caught off guard.

"Yes... Yes, I am." She replied. "I'm Mary Hamilton." Janet recognised her as a close friend from a long time ago when she lived with Jack in the Shetland capital, Lerwick. It was Ham's turn to stare; he stared at Janet. Janet turned and introduced Ham, "This is my father Hamish, he married my mother Margaret, who was Jack and Janet's daughter. I am so surprised you can still see the family resemblance. Some people say I take after my father," she smiled.

"Oh, I am so glad to have the son-in-law and grand-daughter of my best friend staying at my house. We must meet up for a chat while you are here." Janet placed her arm around the landlady's shoulder and guided her away from the door as she did so; she gently took the keys and threw them over her shoulder at the group of men.

"I would love to, but you see…" Janet leaned in conspiratorially, "my father is an important scientist and needs a lot of quiet to focus on his work. He works for the government you see, and those two men are his bodyguards. It's all very hush-hush stuff, so you mustn't tell anyone. I must stay with him as his secretary, and the poor old boy is not that well. That's why we're here. He needs time to focus, the poor guy. Never been the same since mum died. You understand I'm sure?"

"Poor chap. Yes, of course. My number is on the hall table if you need anything. Your grandmother was such a nice lady. Goodbye, dear." And with that, she was off, muttering away to herself.

"Government scientist! Bodyguards! The whole bloody island will know we're here by the end of the day. And I'm your father am I? Bloody cheek!"

"The island knows we're here already. It's a small place. This way, they will leave us alone and give us room to breathe. Orcadians respect privacy."

They checked out the house, a four-bedroom detached house with an attached garage. The nearest house, croft or farm was miles away, well out of sight. They unpacked their equipment and the provisions they had bought at Morrison's in Largs before they had started their journey and made themselves comfortable.

The weather forecast said rain for later that night, so Ham took Major out for a walk. Rob went with him, just in case. Ham appreciated the gesture, but knew that he was safe, the nuckelavee never wandered further inland than the beach when it rained because it could not stand freshwater. It also worked out well for Ham because he wanted John to have time to fly the helicopter up to Wick and to be on call there.

As he walked back to the house, Ham got that itch, the one that said someone was watching them.

Hide and Seek in the Dark

When they got back, Ham told Rob and Jaimie to get as much rest as possible, because he wanted them to go out that night and see who was watching them. They nodded and wandered off to their room, only coming down when Janet called up that diner was ready, fish of course. If Janet was cooking, it was always fish, luckily, she was a good cook and had a fair-sized repertoire of culinary delights.

Dressed in black clothing with darkened faces, carrying matt black or dull coloured equipment, they slid out of the unlit kitchen door into the night rain. Jaimie spotted the car, but Rob spotted the person. He had moved forward from the parked car to where he could see the house. The rain was a nuisance, but through their HMNVS or Head Mounted Night Vision System; they could see him scanning the property. He used a commercial night vision system, functional, but not as good. Night vision or not, the SBS operators knew how to stalk their prey without being seen. They watched him return to his car and place the night vision system down on the passenger side. It looked like he was alone, but they checked anyway. He was alone, so they moved stealthily forward, not making a sound, not being seen. Despite the rain, the driver's side window was ajar, leaving a gap for any sound to enter. This man was no fool if one of the cars had started, he would have heard it.

They came from the rear blind spot, Jaimie to the passenger side and Rob to the driver's side. Jaimie tapped his machine pistol on the passenger side window, then pointed it directly at the driver. A shocked look of panic crossed his face. It grew more so when Rob yanked open the driver's door and grabbing hold of the driver, pulled him forcibly out and down to the floor onto his belly. A Glock 19 pistol pressed against his head.

"Arms out straight! Don't look at me! Cross your legs! I said, don't look at me!" Jaimie came round and took each arm, in turn, brought them behind his back and tied them together firmly with heavy-duty plastic pull-ties. With that done, Rob pulled a black cloth bag over the driver's head. Jaimie searched him thoroughly, starting at the head and finishing with his shoes, while Rob stood guard.

"I'm going to roll you onto you back! Follow my instructions! Sit up! Put your legs under your backside! Now! I am going to lift and turn you! Now, move!" With the prisoner between them, they frog-marched him towards the house. They took him in and straight to the kitchen where they sat him on a chair.

They threw his belongings onto the kitchen table. After a few moments, they took the hood off.

"So, Sgt. James Reid, what brings you out on a night like this?" Ham asked cordially. Jim Reid looked around quickly from one person to another. If he got out of this alive, he wanted to remember each face, each clue to their identity. He looked on the table and saw his warrant card lying there.

"I'm a police officer."

"Yes, I know. It says so on your warrant card. Why were you spying on us?"

"I was not spying... I was observing."

"Potato, potato. Why were you observing us?" asked, still in a calm voice.

"Who are you?" Reid asked. Reid looked around again, two men in black combat uniforms, two women in their twenties in casual clothes, a much older man with a grey-white beard who was doing all the talking, cat that was licking its bum and a dog with metal teeth; metal teeth for God's sake. "Sergeant, sergeant, look here. Why were you 'observing' us?" Ham waited. Reid did not talk.

"Alison, call the general and ask him nicely to call the Chief Constable of Police Scotland. Tell him that we may have one of his men here, but all we have for proof is a warrant card I could manufacture in five minutes. Ask the chief constable to call your number so he can talk to this guy." Macduff started to punch the number out on her phone.

"Stop, stop. Show me some ID. Let me know who you are, and we can talk." Ham thought for a moment, nodded and took out his MI5 ID, and held it in front of Reid.

"Drug Squad. I'm with the drug squad." Ham motioned for Rob to cut Reid's restraints. When he was free, he rubbed his wrists to get the circulation back. They had been tight.

"So why were you observing us? We have nothing to do with drugs?"

I heard that Mrs. Monroe had a booking for a party to rent her old house. It's the wrong season for birdwatchers or climbers. So I picked you up at Thurso and followed you across to Hoy. I watched you on the ferry. An older man in charge, two ladies with a couple of heavies, it didn't fit the profile of your average holiday party." Ham pursed his lips together and nodded a couple of times in agreement. Encouraged Reid continued, "We have a problem with drugs coming from Scotland to the Orkney and Shetland Mainland. I thought you might be bringing stuff across.

"Seems reasonable. Right, I would like a mug of tea. I don't know what the sergeant wants, but I did see you, Rob, buying some whisky earlier. Pity they don't have duty free shops when you land here, anyway, I suggest you put your kit away and get yourself cleaned up. Sergeant, have you eaten?" Jim Reid shook his head at the sudden turn of events. In a quiet voice, Ham muttered to him, "It's going to be fish." He did not understand the significance; he just carried on rubbing his wrists.

Night Swim

"Are you based on the Scottish Mainland?" A nod. "Do you have something here arranged for the night?" A shake. "Excellent, you can stay here the night and make sure we are not up to any skullduggery."

"I have to call in, or they will send someone to find out what happened to me," Reid stated. "my phone's in the car. I'll have to go and get it." Ham smiled. To be honest, smiling was something relatively new to Ham. For most of his adult life, he had restrained his emotions, and a smile was alien on his face. The smile he wore at that moment somehow seemed artificial, menacing.

"Of course, Jaimie has brought your car over; it's outside." Reid looked up; he had not heard Hamilton give any order and was not aware that Jaimie had left the house at any time. He got up and began to walk outside.

"It's Hamilton, Colonel Hamish Hamilton. Good luck with that." The menacing smile reappeared as Ham sipped his mug of tea. Jim Reid went out to his car, sat in the driver's seat and called his boss. His boss answered, told him what the computer said and told him to be very careful. The detective sergeant took his phone and an overnight case he kept in the boot and returned to the house. As he re-entered the kitchen, Ham raised an eyebrow.

"It's above my bosses security level. He can't get access."

"I'm afraid I don't think there is anyone in the Police Scotland who has high enough access to find out. Don't worry about it."

"Janet, let's take this hound for a walk before we turn in for tonight. Bring your wet skin; it'll be wet outside." Janet nodded; she went to get her rucksack and followed. A jangle of the chain, send the dog and cat scurrying out the kitchen door.

"The cat too?" Reid asked.

"They are inseparable, you know," Jaimie answered. "Come on; I'll show you which is your room. I'll move my kit in with Rob." As Jaimie showed Reid upstairs, Ham, Janet and the beasts walked along the road which was parallel to the sea.

"I need you to go in and look for some things under the water. Are you okay to do that this evening, now?" Janet nodded and started to look for a likely spot to enter the water. Finding a suitable spot, she walked off the road towards the water's edge.

"What am I looking for?" she asked.

"Bodies. The bodies that the grave robbers took. I think they are tempting the nuckelavee out of the water by giving it the taste for human flesh. When it's eaten the bodies and wants more, it comes out on land."

"Yeuk! Horrible creatures!" exclaimed Janet.

"Yes. I'd like you if you don't mind, to go in and find the bodies if they are there, and we'll take it from there. Please be very careful; the nuckelavee is very dangerous."

"You forget, I know these waters. And I even think I know in which area it will be." He looked at her. "I said, I think; I shall have to test my theory."

Out of more of a habit than necessity, she looked up and down the road before she started to strip off her clothes. As she did so,

Ham took her seal skin out of the rucksack she had carried. She felt no shame or false modesty standing naked in front of Ham; he had seen her naked many times. Although over two hundred years old in human years, she had the body and features of a twenty-five-year-old, a very beautiful and voluptuous twenty-five-year-old and she knew it.

"Come on, stop parading yourself and get yourself into this," Ham said, holding up her seal skin. Janet gave a little pout and took the proffered skin. She wrapped the skin around her body, and she became a seal. There was no flash or thundered, no moaning and groaning as her features changed, one minute she was a woman wrapped in a seal's skin and the next she was a seal sliding to the floor.

"I'll take your clothes with me. Princess will tell me when you are ready to come back." Janet, in seal form, turned awkwardly and flopped into the sea. Ham watch where she had been for a moment and then walked back to the house.

Major, realising that they were heading back to the house, piddled a couple of times, enough to see him through the night. Princess, being a smart little thing, realised that no-one had remembered to bring her cat box, so she squatted and relieved herself as well. Ham dutifully waited for them both to finish, and then the three of them walked back to the house.

Barrel of Butter

Jaimie and Rob were in the kitchen, Jim Reid came down and joined them.

"I could smell the cooking," Reid said.

"Do you want an egg banjo?"

"A what?"

"What's an egg banjo?" The two SBS operators laughed. The policeman looked puzzled. "Ok, stand there." Reid did so, a puzzled look on his face. "Now, hold an imaginer fried egg sandwich in both hands as if you are eating it." He did so with a puzzled look on his face. "Great, now this egg sandwich has lovely runny egg yolk, what's going to happen?"

"It'll dribble."

"What do you do?" Reid lifted the egg sandwich out of the way with his right hand and wiped his shirt with his left.

"Da-da-da-dah- dah-dah-da-dah[2]." The two SBS men made banjo music sounds in unison and laughed. The policeman looked at his pose and realised that he looked as if he were playing the air banjo and laughed as well. It was while they were laughing that the front door opened. Through the open kitchen door, they could see Janet. She closed the door and walked into the kitchen. She was stark naked, save a sealskin fur which she held under her arm. The operators, although surprised at her sudden naked appearance, did their best to appear as if everything was normal. Jim Reid's jaw dropped. He stared at Janet and then at the two men.

"Where is he?" The two operators pointed upstairs silently. The policeman continued to stare. This behaviour was not normal in the Orkney Islands

She turned and left the room; moments later, they heard her ascend the stairs. Her footsteps were heavy; she was upset.

"Somebody is going to get it." Stated Jaimie. Rob nodded silently.

---

[2] Normally the banjo music from the film Deliverence is sung by military personnel during the explanation, but as military people tend to be tone deaf any general banjo sounds suffices.

"So, you want a banjo?" Rob said to Reid. The policeman pointed towards the kitchen door and waited for an explanation. None came. He nodded.

"Good, take a seat. Tea or coffee?"

Ham woke to find Janet standing in his doorframe, naked apart from the seal fur looped over her arms, with her arms firmly planted on her hips. She did not look happy; Ham looked tired. Major looked from one to the other with a puzzled expression on his face.

"You were supposed to meet me with my clothes."

"I expected Princess to tell me when you were ready to come out as she normally does. Where is she anyway? You're back quicker than I thought." He protested. "Go and clean up and report back to me here. Major go and find your sister." Major got up and left. Janet glared once more at Ham and followed Major out of the door. Oops, thought Ham.

Fifteen, twenty minutes later, Janet returned to Ham's room. By then, Ham was dressed and awake. He sat on the bed and signalled Janet to sit beside him.

"Sorry, you were quicker than I thought you'd be, what did you find out?"

"I found the bodies weighted down with anchors or chains around the Barrel of Butter in the Scapa Flow."

"Barrel of Butter?" queried Ham with a puzzled look on his face.

"A small island in Skapa Flow, it used to be called, Carlin Skerry, but some seal hunters from Orphir rented the island for the rent of a barrel of butter every year from the local laird. It is a place where seals congregate; therefore, it is the place where the nuckelavee, who eat seals, would go."

"How many bodies did you find?"

"Six in various states of decay and being eaten. But, that is not the important part..." Ham waited. "While I was there, a boat came and dropped another one." She described the boat including its registration number painted on its hull and the men on the boat.

"Well done. Very well done. Let's go downstairs for some breakfast. You go first. I'll join you shortly." He stood up and held his hand out to help Janet up. Janet looked at his proffered hand, then at him, and then smiled wryly and accepted the hand. She shook her head and went downstairs, entering the kitchen. Reid focused on his mug; he seemed to be having problems looking at Janet.

"Nothing like a good skinny-dip first thing in the morning," exclaimed Janet. The operators said nothing. It was at this moment that Major returned with Princess hanging in his jaws and from her jaws hung a rabbit about twice her size.

"Princess!" exclaimed Janet, "you let that poor animal go!" Princess's eyes moved, but the rabbit remained in place. Major spat out Princess, as she landed, the rabbit fell out of her mouth and took off. The kitchen door was open, but the rabbit decided to run under the table and chairs. Princess followed and the humans tried to catch the rabbit or the cat. Major sat with a bemused expression on his face watching the strange goings-on.

Eye in the Sky

When Ham had finished his phone call to the general, he too came downstairs to the kitchen.

"What was all the kerfuffle about?" he asked; nodding to Rob who lifted a mug in question.

"Princess thought she was a tiger and brought home her prey, rabbit." Jaimie flipped a thumb out the kitchen door to the outside. Ham scowled at the cat, which ignored the gesture, it was beneath its dignity.

"Sergeant Reid I have one of those 'good news, bad news' scenarios for you." Reid looked back at him in a puzzled questioning manner.

"Ok colonel, let's have it." Ham took his coffee from Rob and sat down at the table.

"Last night the RAF had a training exercise for one of their MQ-9A Reaper MALE, medium-altitude long-endurance, aircraft, I think you would call it a drone, out of RAF Waddington. It seems that while it was flying around up there," he waved a thumb in the general direction, "it followed a small boat from Thurso up here to Scapa Flow. It also monitored this boat land, and then return to Thurso. Now, these drones are damn good, probably much better than you've seen in newsreels of Afghanistan or Iraq. As part of its training, it captured the boat's name, full face shots of the three men on board; it captured a lovely video of them offloading some packages and of course, the men receiving and their vehicle number plate." Ham could see Reid's excitement grow, so he held up his hand before he continued.

"And now for the bad news..." Reid's excitement seemed to deflate a little. "You need to take the ferries and go back to Thurso. Report to the police station tomorrow; there you will be met by a couple of Special Branch officers. They will have all the photos and videos and if they are any good, the names and details of the suspects, involved in last night's little boat ride; if not, you'll have to sort that part out. You'll arrest the people involved on narcotic charges. You will get the bust or whatever you call it, but and here's the catch, the Special Branch officers will take the suspects away, they won't go through the normal booking in procedure. When the Special Branch have concluded their business with them there'll be a trial, but 'in camera', the general public won't learn about the drones, we were not here, and you've never heard of us or anything like that. As the arresting officer, you will, of course, attend the trial and you'll see justice done. It will all be very legal." Ham raised his hands and shrugged his shoulders as if to say; it's that simple. He could see the look of doubt on Reid's face.

"Ring your superior in about an hour for confirmation, about the Special Branch officers. They won't know about the rest. You've signed the Official Secrets Act. Need I say more?" Reid shook his head.

The Stalking

It was about mid-day when Sgt. Jim Reid drove off with much waving and smiles. The team returned to the kitchen to plan that evening's entertainment. The weather forecast was good, and Ham expected a visitor to Hoy that night.

When it was dark, the two cars drove north to the north-east side of the island nearer the Skapa Flow, the probable landing site of the nuckelavee. They parked in a quiet spot away from dwellings and waited. Macduff checked the communications and put on the loudspeaker for Janet. Janet was the only one not wearing a headset and mic.

"Yes, I see you Mike India One. I have good vision. Are you aware that you have another vehicle nearby; he followed you from Lyness Bay and is parked about a thousand meters back from where you are?"

"Oversight Four[3]. Thank you for the information. Keep us informed of the vehicle and its occupant actions. Mark as Romeo One. Do not treat as hostile but keep under observation."

"That'll be bloody Reid; I bet," Macduff muttered aloud, Ham slowly nodded in agreement.

"Mike India One, Oversight Four, we have a movement on the beach near Romeo One. It looks like a horse and rider are leaving the water about a hundred meters behind Romeo One. Mike India One?"

"Oversight Four, Mike India One, mark as Tango One. And advise what it's doing?"

"Mike India One, do I mark as Tango One and Two?" Ham, snorted.

"Macduff, turn around and head back quickly." To the throat microphone, he said, "negative Oversight Four, mark both as Tango One." As Macduff started to turn, he looked across at the car containing the two SBS operators. "Mike India Three and Four, you

_____

[3] In this operation Oversight Four was an unmanned Reaper from RAF Waddington. Reaper will be replaced by Predator B.

heard, follow us." As the other vehicle also reversed direction, Ham used the Throat Mike again. "Mike India Five, Mike India One, lift-off and rendezvous at Tango One location."

"Mike India One, Tango is stalking Romeo One. Romeo One has left the vehicle, marked Romeo Two, and is walking towards you. Tango One is seventy-five meters and gaining on Romeo One. Romeo One seems unaware of Tango One at this time. Tango One is at Romeo Two, fifty meters and gaining on Romeo One. Romeo One still walking towards you. Romeo One is still unaware that Tango One is behind him and closing, approximately twenty plus meters. Directly in front of you, Mike India One."

Just as Macduff was about to apply the brakes, the car driven by Rob shot past them and spun into a halt across the road just in front of Reid. Sergeant Reid, caught unawares by the sudden appearance of the vehicle in front, froze. Rob and Jaimie exited the car even as it stopped; both raised their rifles in unison. Reid started to raise his hands; he thought he was the focus of their attention.

"Get down, Jim! Jim, get down, now!" came the slightly muffled voice from behind the gas mask. Reid started to comply, Rob and Jaimie fired together. Both reloaded and fired again. All four darts struck the nuckelavee. The creature plucked the darts out and stared at them as the two operatives raised their machine pistols ready to fire. Their gloved trigger fingers took first pressure and waited.

"Darts! Give it two more darts!" shouted Ham through his gas mask as he ran up to the car. Macbeth was right behind him, holding her machine pistol ready. The two operators released the machine pistols, which swung away on their harness, and quickly reloaded the tranquilliser rifles. As they brought the rifles up to bear, the creature started to fall forward. As it fell an evil-smelling noxious smoke belched from its throat enveloping Sergeant Reid, who clutched his throat and fell back from where he had been kneeling.

"Damn," muttered Ham.

"Golf India One, Mike India One, we need immediate casevac[4] of Romeo One from Kirkwall to Newquay, I repeat, Newquay, to visit Magic One. Romeo is Romeo Echo India Delta. We will need the vehicle in Newquay, so arrange vehicle entrance at Kirkwall and Vehicle exit and later entrance at Newquay. We will also need the ferry from Moaness, Hoy to the Stromness, Orkney Island Mainland ASAP[5]. Understood?"

"Mike India One, Golf India One, understood. I have a Charlie 130 Juliet from 47 Squadron[6] waiting at RAF Lossiemouth," replied the general. Ms. Miller, who was next to him, was already on the telephone making arrangements.

"Mike India One, Golf India One, what is the situation with Romeo One?"

"Golf India One, Mike India One, he's got Mortasheen[7] Disease, repeat Mortasheen. Understood?

"Understood" came the simple resigned reply.

The team on the island carefully removed the gas masks. There was still a faint foul smell, but the wind had dissipated most of it.

---

[4] Casualty Evacuation
[5] As Soon As Possible
[6] Part of UK Special Forces Aviation Wing
[7] Deadly disease originating from the toxic breathe of the nuckelavee

"Oversight Four, Mike India One, Mike India Five en route, follow to drop-off, then End-Op. Acknowledge?"

Mike India One, Oversight Four, acknowledge."

"Rob, Jaimie get the tarpaulin out and gift wrap our friend here. Transport's on the way. They know where to take it. If anyone comes in the meantime, it's a horse that was hit by a car, and you are airlifting to a vet. Try not to look so military; you'll scare the natives. When they've gone, go back to the house and sterilise it like we were never there. Take the next available ferry and go home. Ok?"

"Ok, boss. What about him?" Rob said, pointing at Reid. "He doesn't look too good."

"I've got him," Macduff said, walking over and hauling Reid up. She carried him to the car and shoved him onto the back seat next to Janet. The three men looked at each other. "What? Do you think a girl can't do that? I lift weights." She went to the driver's door and got in. When she knew that they could not see, she turned to Janet and smiled. Ham got in the passenger seat, and they drove

off north.

Mither o' the Sea

As Ham waited for the ferry to the Orkney Mainland, an AS365N3 Dauphin helicopter from number 658 Squadron AAC[8] JSFAW[9] in its dark civilian like colours landed next to where Rob and Jaimie had trussed up the nuckelavee in a tarpaulin. John exited the helicopter dragging a net and cable along behind him. The two went to help him, and they rolled the nuckelavee onto the net which was then drawn together with a cable like a purse.

"I thought you were supposed to be flying the helicopter?" asked Rob.

"These Army Air Corp pilots get quite touchy about their aircraft, especially the 658 Squadron guys. Threatened to shoot me if I tried, so I let him fly." Grinned John.

John ran back to the helicopter and attached the other end of the cable to the aircraft. He waved to his team-mates and climbed aboard.

---

[8] Army Air Corp.
[9] Joint Special Forces Aviation Wing based at Credenhill, Herefordshire.

The helicopter rose and hovered over the creature, John hanging half out of the door, guiding the pilot, gradually it took the strain and then lifted the nuckelavee into the air. When it had gained sufficient height, it headed north over the Scapa Flow and the Orcadian Mainland towards the Fair Isle, a Shetland island lying halfway between the Shetland and Orkney Mainland's.

As it drew near to the South Lighthouse, it turned left towards the Atlantic Ocean. About five kilometres out, the helicopter came to a hover, then slowly lowered the net down towards the sea. John released the cable, and the creature fell out of the net and tarpaulin into the sea. Somewhere beneath the sea lived the only living thing that could control the nuckelavee, the Mither of the Sea, the Orcadian summer spirit that fought all winter with Teran the winter spirit. The nuckelavee being a creature of Teran was the natural enemy of Mither, she would fight to control it as part of her annual fight for control of the Orkney Islands. The nuckelavee would not return to the Orkney Islands at least for that year; Ham knew Mither would see to that.

A thumbs up to the pilot and the Dauphin turned and headed south to RM Condor near Arbroath where John had left his car.

Merlin's Magic

When they arrived at Kirkwall Airport, they flashed their IDs and drove straight through the gate onto airside. The Hercules was waiting with the ramp down and the engines running. Ham directed Macduff to drive straight up, into the aircraft, as she entered, she was guided by the warrant officer Air LoadMaster to the correct spot. As the 'loadie' started to chain down the vehicle for the flight, another member of the aircrew was preparing and raising the ramp. Even as the ramp was raising the aircraft started to move.

The aircraft quickly took off and headed south towards Cornwall. Once they levelled off, the loadie brought them paper cups of coffee. The loadie noticed sergeant Reid half lying, half sitting on the back seat; he asked Ham if they wanted a blanket for him, which Ham accepted. The loadie did not say anything else. On these types of flights, you did not ask questions.

The runway at Newquay Airport splits the old RAF St Mawgan on one side and the civilian Newquay airport on the other. Flight operations at the RAF base had long since stopped, but if the aircraft had taxied and parked on the RAF side, it would have been a five-kilometre journey round to the airfield to St Mawgan village and down the valley to the Enchanted Forest. When they landed, the aircraft taxied directly to the civilian side. It was less than a kilometre from there to their destination. As the aircraft landed and taxied at Newquay, the loadie undid the chain holding the car in place, as the ramp lowered, this was not the normal practise on RAF transport aircraft, but the aircrew were not virgins to special forces operations. The aircraft came to a halt, and the car revered off and drove to the gate which was being held open for them. Ham waved his thanks and they again headed towards the valley and down to the Enchanted Forest and the wizard's house.

There had been no stag on guard, but Ambrose was waiting for them with a worried look on his face.

"Bring him indoors straight away," Ambrose ordered. There was no humour or playfulness in his eyes; he was deadly serious. Macduff and Janet carried Reid indoors and lay him on the couch as directed by Ambrose. The wizard quickly examined the police sergeant's eyes, lips, nails and wrists. "Mortasheen," muttered Ambrose as he disappeared through the kitchen door. Everyone, including the animals, waited.

It was ten to fifteen minutes before Ambrose returned with a bright pink solution in a porcelain bowl. He knelt next to the couch and dipped a clean white cloth into the mixture. He paused, stood up and handed the two items to Janet.

"Here selkie, wipe his face, neck hands and anything exposed to the nuckelavee's breath with this mixture. Keep applying it. Ambrose returned to the kitchen.

Janet applied the solution until Ambrose returned a short while later with a dark brown liquid.

"Raise him," Ambrose instructed. He then gently poured the liquid into Reid's mouth. Reid did not react. Ambrose muttered to himself and left the room again with a worried look on his face.

Ambrose walked in and stood over Reid but looking at Ham, "I believe this will work. By that, I mean that it will save his life, but there is a heavy caveat. There is a price he may not be willing to pay. If this does not work…" He left the sentence incomplete. Ham nodded slowly.

"He needs to live Merlin," Ham said quietly forgetting to call him Ambrose. "He is a good man. Go ahead." Ambrose knelt and began to ladle a green liquid into Reid's slack mouth. Immediately after the third spoonful, Ambrose pushed the wooden spoon's handle sideways into Reid's mouth. He only just made it. Reid suddenly arched upwards violently with a deep groan in his throat. Ambrose held the spoon forcible in Reid's mouth, if he had not, Reid would have bitten his tongue or crushed his teeth.

"Hold him down!" Shouted the wizard. They were all suddenly galvanised; Janet took his legs, while Macduff took hold of his arms. Ham held his body. The animals left the house as if unable to watch.

Reid bucked and strained for what seemed like ages but was only minutes. Eventually, he slumped back onto the couch, his whole body covered in sweat. Slowly his breathing became regular, and his eyes flickered open.

"Wow!" he exclaimed with a croaky voice. "Wow, what a rush."

"Jesus," muttered Ham. Ham turned to Ambrose and asked, "How is he, Ambrose?"

"He will live, but there is that caveat I mentioned," Ambrose stated sadly. "He can live a long and full life, much longer than most mortals, but he must remain in the Enchanted Forest." They all looked at Ambrose incredulously.

"What? You didn't say anything about that." Spluttered Ham.

"There wasn't time Hamish. The last potion I gave him, saved his life, but only as long as he lives in the Enchanted Forest. If he leaves, he will die within three months. To a doctor, it will look like cancer, but it is the mortasheen." Turning to Jim Reid, he continued, "If you leave here, it is with a death sentence on your head. I am sorry, but it was the only way to save you." Reid hung his head.

"I have a wife and child," he said softly. "I cannot remain here."

"If you go back you know what will happen," Ham said.

Yes, I will get my arrest, I will get my life in order, and I can say farewell to my family." He looked up at Ambrose, "Thank you for giving me this time. When can I leave?" Macduff fought back her tears, Ham's eyes were glassy, but Janet stood stoic, selkies viewed life and death differently.

"As soon as you can get out of my house," the wizard replied with an understanding smile. "I suggest you remember the way here in case you change your mind. It is an option; it is the only one I can offer. Enjoy your family, young man. Your daughter will grow into a beautiful and intelligent woman." Reid nodded his thanks. Ham had stopped trying to guess how Merlin knew things, many years ago.

Half an hour after leaving Ambrose with heavy hearts, they were in the air, drinking coffee and heading north to Kirkwall. The loadie noticed that the previously sick man was wet but healthy, but he said nothing; he did offer another blanket.

While in the Enchanted Forest, Ham had seen Reid's life force on a scale that was off the charts, but as soon as they left, he saw it fall away to indicate only a few months.

On their arrival, they drove down to Reid's car, which he assured them he was capable of driving. Janet insisted that she would drive to be safe. Reid remembered Janet naked in the kitchen, and his face flushed the whole journey. They followed him to the ferry and then to Thurso police station where the Special Branch officers, who were in fact MIC interrogators met them.

Ham took Reid to one side and again re-emphasised the need for secrecy. Reid said that he did not understand what had been going on, but of course, he would never talk of it; for as long as he lived.

The Deception

For the next two days, nothing special happened, John, returned to his flat from Arbroath, Jaimie and Rob returned from their housecleaning chores, and Ham and the rest returned from Kirkwall.

Police Sgt. Reid met up with the Special Branch officers and arrested the grave robbers and drug smugglers. The Special Branch officers whisked the suspects away, only to return three very compliant suspects three days later to Thurso police station. The trial was as Ham had predicted held in camera[10], with the public kept at bay. The judge commended Sergeant Reid for freeing Northern Scotland from this criminal menace. Pleading guilty the culprits received relatively light sentences, and Sergeant Reid returned to police duties until the end.

Ham walked every morning and evening with the beasts, brooding over the recent events, convinced that the whole

---

[10] In secret, filmed for legal record, but no public or press allowed

nuckelavee incident was a side-show, a distraction from the main event, but he could not see what that was.

The answer started to come on the third day after a phone call from the general. Following their quiet chat with the MIC investigators, the Thurso grave-robbers cum drug smugglers, described their employer, as a brash, stocky clean-shaven American with gold-rimmed glasses, working out of Canada.

Why would Colonel Maddox want to be in Canada? Ham knew. He dreaded the answer, but he knew.

Brunch at Green Shutters

After his phone call with the general, Ham walked slowly back from the boating pond area towards his flat on Fort Street; his head tucked into his turned-up collar out of the slight rain. The road was quiet and Major ran ahead off the leash, his fur covered in a fine coating of rain droplets, but this time Ham wanted to walk and think some more. It took a few moments for the dog to realise that he was alone at the street door to the flat, he looked around and saw Ham still walking along the promenade under the multi-coloured illuminations, and past the closed Green Shutters. Major loped after him and fell into step. Princess popped her head out of the rucksack Ham carried on his back and looked around. She meowed a couple of times and returned disinterestedly to her dry, warm, cosy, temporary sleeping place.

Just past the Green Shutters, but only just, there is a ramp leading down to the shore, and next to the ramp there is a semi-circular bulge in the promenade pointing out over the river towards the Isle of Cumbrae. He walked to the railing and took up his normal thinking posture, resting his elbows on the railings, and staring out into the void. He was not admiring the view; he was many years in the past and thousands of miles away. Major sat and then lay beside him, seemingly deep in his thoughts. Major was more aware of his surroundings, and his ears would follow the occasional passer-by, nobody came near enough to arouse his interest.

Ham took his mobile phone out and called the team together for brunch the next day.

"Be there before 11.30 am if you want breakfast, after that it's the day menu, no square sausage or bacon rolls. I'll take Major out earlier and make reservations."

The next morning, they were all there at eleven, as Ham guessed they would be, the sausage and bacon rolls were good. Even Janet, who did not, as a rule, eat meat arrived early for her morning coffee.

"Ok boys and girls enjoy your breakfast because you are going to be busy for the rest of the day.

Nakanni and Friends

After breakfast, they retired to Ham's apartment. In the living room, Ham opened the buro and took out a small electronic device which he handed to Macduff.

"Scan this room first, then all the others," he said. Macduff looked at the device, nodded and set to work.

"Rob, John, Jamie, one of you make tea and coffee for everyone; you can fight for that privilege, the other two search this place for anything that the scanner might miss. What we are about to discuss is for your ears only, understand?" Jaimie headed to the kitchen; the other two started searching the living room systematically. It was a small one-bedroom flat, so it didn't take them long. The coffee was still warm.

"Right, make yourselves comfortable, because I am about to give you a little history lesson, about something that will never appear in any history book." He paused while he gathered his thoughts and then he began.

"In the early nineteen-seventies in North America, there were a lot of sasquatches, bigfoots, skunk-apes, Canadian yellow-top sightings. Humans were crowding into their areas, and it was only going to be a matter of time before one or more were killed or captured. You know what would have happened then, open season for trophy hunters. At the same time, the American army wanted to capture these beasts to militarise them. Can you imagine an army of sasquatch in the field?"

"Jack Drummond, that's Janet late husband, by the way, John and my immediate boss, myself and a chap called Simon Hunter were sent to hunt, round up and move the sasquatch family to a sanctuary. We had to locate and move the skunk-ape from Florida, the sasquatch or bigfoot from Oregon, Northern California and Washington State in America and British Columbia in Canada, yellow-top we also had to move from Ontario, Canada. Because the Americans under then Captain Maddox were also hunting the sasquatch, it was all done in absolute secrecy. The mission was a joint operation with the then RCMP; Royal Canadian Mounted

Police Security Service Department C. The Americans were our allies and it would not have been done for them to find out. It was all done very surreptitiously and over many years." Ham sniggered a bit. "There were a lot of UFO sightings during this period, that was probably us. There was a lot of sneaking about and skulduggery, but we managed it in the end. And that is why you hardly get a bigfoot sighting these days."

"Where did you put them?" asked Macduff. She looked at Ham, and he seemed to struggle with the answer. She realised that this was one of the department's biggest secrets.

"Some sasquatch, bigfoot or whatever you want to call them, already live in the Mckenzie Region in the Canadian Northwest Territories, near what is known as the Nahanni National Park, there they are known as the nakanni by the Naha people. The Nahas disappeared from public view many years ago, but they are still there, they only come out of their caves at night and more importantly they revere the nakanni. They have been protecting the nakanni for hundreds of years. Once we made contact, we were able to convince them to adopt the other members of the nakanni family. It was not easy as the Naha people have a bad habit of removing the heads of anyone who gets too close to their beloved nakanni. There is an area near where we are going called, the Valley of the Headless Men. Now, isn't that something to look forward to?"

"Now to planning, the general is aware of what we have to do, so has already made some arrangements. Here is what I want you to do, Macduff, contact Ms. Miller on the general's staff and arrange transport and liaison with the Canadian Special Forces of Intelligence Branch, Ms. Miller will know which. I don't want to fly into any of the bases with any joint American operation, like CFB, Canadian Forces Base Gander, we fly from RAF Brize Norton to CFB Trenton initially. Trenton is big enough and we can maybe blend in with the other flights. It's important, keep us away from the Americans and civilians. Colonel Maddox may be a civilian and freelancing, but I'm sure he still has friends and informants inside the American military."

"Maddox?" queried Macduff. "I thought we killed him at Eilean Nan Creagan11

"I wish we had, but I'm afraid he is very much alive and is behind that whole business in the Orkneys. He meant it as a distraction. While we were messing about with the nuckelavee, he was going north to search the Nahanni Valley."

John, Rob, Jaimie, work out what equipment you think we will need, the whole team. The weather there is still in the minus twenty-five or so at this time of the year. But bear in mind there are areas in the Nahanni Valley that are tropical all the year-round." They stared at him incredulously.

"There are hot springs in the area which supply year-round heat. Snow and blizzards all around and yet in some valleys and sinkholes, you will find a tropical climate. It is there that we will find the Naha and there we will find the sasquatch which we must at all costs protect from Maddox and his gang. I don't know who his paymasters are this time; it could be the North Koreans again, the

---

11 See The Boundary Walker by Deryk Cameron Stronach

Chinese or Russians. Whoever it is, we must protect the creatures. Go away and work out what you need. What we don't have here, Ms Miller will arrange to delivery to Brize Norton.

"Janet, I don't know if you want to come with us on this part of the operation. Apart from a few lakes, there is not much water up there, at least not in the area that we are going. Maybe you should stay here with the beasts."

"That's just the point isn't it Hamish Hamilton. You don't know what to expect. I am part of this team, and I am coming along. I shall give you my measurements later, Rob; I will require the full kit, or whatever you call it."

"Janet, the Canadians still cull seals. What if they catch you as a seal?" It was a cheap shot, but it was worth a try.

"What if I stick a Glock 19 9mm up their nose?" was her reply. Ham rolled his eyes.

"Arriving in Trenton, we shall meet up with our counterparts in CIS, Canadian Intelligence Service, from there we will fly over the Mckenzie region and parachute in. There are no roads, and if you try by the river this time of the year, you are asking for trouble as the area we have to visit is rather dodgy for water landings at the best of times to say the least. Anyway, we will not fly in by floatplane or helicopter because if Maddox is in the area, I don't want to lead him to the valley we are going. Janet, parachute?"

She shrugged her shoulders and said nothing.

"John, we'll be going HAHO[12]. Janet can go tandem with you?" John nodded.

"No problem, boss."

"Rob, you will take Major, and I shall take Princess. Macduff you've only just passed your SF parachute course, and this will not be an easy first operational jump, so I want Jaimie to stay near you." She started to protest, but Ham stared her down. "John I've just had a thought, we will need oxygen for Major. Major will have been trained and I am sure they can get hold on an oxygen mask for him, but I'm sure they have never HAHO'd a cat, see what you can come

---

[12] High Altitude High Opening military parachute insertion, the other being HALO, High Altitude Low Opening.

up with for Princess. I'm not sure what height we are going to jump in from until I talk with the Canadians."

"Sorry boss, but why is Princess coming with us? The Canadian wilderness is not exactly house cat territory," John asked. Princess phutted in disgust and growled.

"To be honest John, it's not exactly old retired colonel's territory either. She comes because she is part of the team. She may be useful; she has been in the past. Who would look after her while we were away?" John shrugged. Princess turned away in a snooty manner.

"Make sure you chose your weapons carefully; there is no popping back to the armoury for more. Rations, the Canadians will take care that, but check when we arrive. I don't want to be living off moose and beaver during our little excursion. If there is anything I have forgotten and there probably is, take care of it, you are all big boys and girls. One last thing…" There was a pause; all of them looked at Ham. "Thirsty work all this."

Janet took the hint and went to make him a mug of tea. "Add tea to the list of things to take." She muttered to Rob as she passed.

Across the Water

The drive down from Scotland to England took them most of the night. The two cars arrived at RAF Brize Norton early in the morning. Once on the base, Ham led the way to the gate near the Air Movements Cargo hanger where they were met by some waiting RAF Policemen and escorted airside to a 70 Squadron A400M Atlas parked on an outside position away from the passenger terminal.

While the others loaded their equipment on board, Ham got Macduff to check the supplies delivered from Ms Miller. Ham took the two beasts to one side where Major relieved himself on the grass and Princess getting the idea, did the same. Ham asked the police if the poo had to be removed from the grass as he certainly wasn't going to take it with him. The policeman said he would check with the 'poodle-pushers', the dog handlers, and let them deal with it.

After they had loaded their kit which the 'movers' strapped and netted down securely, they handed over the keys to their cars to the RAFPs who, as agreed beforehand, would park them securely until their return. John had a quiet word with the SNCO[13] that they should not explore the vehicles too much and that secure meant secure even from the RAFPs.

With everyone safely aboard the aircrew raised the ramp, the aircraft taxied, and they were off to CFB Trenton in Ontario, Canada via the Great Circle Route over Southern Greenland.

The journey was noisy but comfortable. Ham's team were the only passengers, but the RAF had loaded some cargo for Trenton. This cargo was to the team's advantage, as it made the slinging of hammocks using spare cargo nets easier. Jaimie showed Janet how to click the metal clasps, scattered around the net for securing cargo, fixing the nets between the cargo pallets. The loadie laid out a blanket for the beasts where they stayed for most of the journey. Major was wearing a military harness, and one custom-built for Princess was worn proudly but reluctantly by the feline. Proudly when she walked beside Major, but reluctantly when Ham pulled her back from a little aircraft exploring.

---

[13] Senior Non-Commissioned Officer.

RAF inflight meals are not known for their gourmet qualities, but they did fill a gap and also a bit of the time. There were no inflight movies; everything was very basic. Nobody brought noise-cancelling earphones or headsets as they were going operational after landing.

Rob and Jaimie slept in their 'green slugs', sleeping bags on their 'hammocks' for most of their journey. John read an old tattered and torn paperback. Janet and Macduff slept fitfully, waking, looking around as if wondering where they were before going back to sleep. Ham spent most of the flight deep in thought; he did, however realising that they would be active as soon as they arrived, manage an occasional cat-nap.

Woken with a cup of coffee shortly before landing, they were stowed away and ready for the landing in plenty of time. The aircraft landed surprisingly gently, and it taxied to a quiet outside position.

The ramp lowered, and they met their arrival committee. Ham stared at the group. By sheer willpower, he controlled expressing his emotions. Major and Princess reacted defensively but for a different reason. Macduff could sense that something was not right, and she looked at the group and then at Ham. Rob and Jaimie knew what was wrong, at least with Ham.

"Boss, you ok?" was all Macduff asked. Ham did his best to smile and nodded slowly.

"Look what is in front of you and control the animals Macduff."

When the ramp had lowered completely, the team walked down and stood in from of the reception committee. The beasts reacted differently; Princess was defensive rearing up and exposing her teeth; Major wanted to get in front of Ham to protect him. Ham signalled for Rob and Macduff to hold back the animals. CFB[14] Trenton was an Airport of Entry; thus a member of the Canada Border Services Agency, walked across to the aircraft. The Canadian officer in charge of the meeting party intercepted the agent and she turned and walked back to her car.

---

[14] Canadian Forces Base

"Ham, so good to see you, my friend. It has been too long. Your pets, it seems they do not like me?" he smiled.

"It's not you Ivor, and you know it." Ivor grinned. Ham shook the proffered hand and introduced Major Ivor Kennedy, a blond-haired giant from the Canadian Intelligence or Int. Branch to his team. The major in turn introduce Ham's team to his team, Captain Ettiene Bouchard, a dark brown haired stocky, bearded man in his early thirties and Sergeant Antonia 'Toni' Morello, a dark-haired smiling woman of Latin descent, both assigned to him from CSOR, or Canadian Special Operations Regiment. There was a pregnant pause before Major Kennedy introduced the other people there.

"Ham, I believe you know, Commander Dave Slaughter, Lieutenant Joe Pottkamp, Chief Petty Officers Sam Wainwright and David 'Not Dave' Apps?" Ham knew Slaughter from previous missions, and the rest of his SEAL team from their recent joint operation releasing the kelpies from Eilean Nan Creagan nodded politely and shook their hands.

"Well, I must say I was not expecting to see you here." Ham looked from the American SEAL team leader to the Canadian major. His face hid his confusion and anger; mostly. The major did not deign to explain the situation at that time. He ushered everyone to some waiting army vehicles.

The Gathering of the Clans

Ham had been at the airbase many times over the years, but those visits or transits had been long ago and of short duration. It had changed enough that he did not recognise the single-story non-descript building where the vehicles came to a halt. Major Kennedy led the way in with Ham, followed by his team, both humans and beasts. The animals were still upset and kept trying to turn around aggressively. Dave Slaughter and the SEAL team found their reaction highly amusing. The rest of the Canadians brought up the rear.

They entered through a wide hallway into a large room with a large wooden table in the centre. Chairs surrounded the table in casual disarray.

Open doorways led off the room in all directions. Ham turned to his team.

"Lads bring the gear inside." he looked at Kennedy. Kennedy raised his arms and pointed in the general direction of the doorways.

"My team are in there; the SEALs are in that one. Pick one from what's left". The operators nodded and left the building.

"I'll help them, boss," stated CPO Apps. Slaughter nodded agreement.

Ham was looking at Major and Princess, who were still agitated.

"Macduff, please take all the beasts out for a walk. All three of them." Macduff looked at Ham in puzzlement; he was normally not so rude towards Janet. Janet smiled at Macduff.

"He does not mean me." She turned and walked towards another doorway. "I'll make some drinks." She knew.

Macduff possessed the second sight, she was a Boundary Walker, the same as Ham, Slaughter and Kennedy, but she was untrained, and her brain was overpowering her instincts. Janet ignored the insult, in fact; she found it amusing, she knew that Ham wanted Macduff to use her second sight; to look around with her ability, rather than just her eyes.

Macduff looked around and stared back at him blankly.

"He means me. Let's take the other animals for a walk. They need to get used to me," smiled Ettiene Bouchard, ushering them out. Macduff looked back at him. He grinned, and she saw an animalistic glint in his eyes. She saw something, but she did not know what. "Loup-garou" he hinted in his French-Canadian accent. She still did not understand. He would explain to her as they walked.

"He's not your plain old loup-garou, is he?" asked Ham, Kennedy smiled back.

"I'll go help the others," said sergeant Morello with a grin.

"Find something to do," suggested Slaughter to the rest of his team. They took the hint and disappeared. Kennedy pointed to a room off to the side. Inside, sat a smaller table and four chairs. Kennedy waved to the other chairs and sat down. Ham waited; he guessed this cosy chat would be interesting

The Open Secret

"I guess we owe you an explanation," Slaughter started. Ham held up his hand. His face was blank, showing neither happiness nor anger with the present situation.

"Hold on a few moments, please." Puzzled Slaughter waited. Kennedy grinned to himself; he knew Ham's habits.

A few minutes later, Janet came in with a tray of four drinks, two coffees for the Canadian and the American and a mug of tea for Ham. She left with one. Ham took a grateful sip and visibly relaxed.

"Now we can talk," he said evenly. Slaughter looked at Kennedy and rolled his eyes.

"You English," he sighed.

"Scottish." Corrected Ham.

"British," compromised Slaughter. Ham nodded and sipped his tea. He held his mug in two hands and peered over the top at the American. He raised his eyebrows to signal that he was ready.

"Many years ago, mid-seventies, while we were running tests on our spy satellite, I believe one may have strayed over Canada, we discovered the valley of the nakanni, your reservation, your bigfoot sanctuary by accident."

Kennedy smirked to show his disbelief in response. "It's a bit like the neighbour's dog shitting in your back garden." Dave Slaughter chose to ignore the comment.

The first thought in Ham's mind was that if the American's knew, why did Colonel Graham, who was in charge of the American cryptid programme at that time, not say or do something about it.

Slaughter continued, "Colonel Graham, sat on it. Although Lieutenant-colonel Maddox was his next in command, he did not tell him, because he did not trust him. He knew that Maddox would hunt the animals in America for his brand of America military usage, weaponising them, something he has tried to do with every cryptid we found. If Maddox ever found out that there was a bigfoot reservation in Canada and that you had filled it with American bigfoot, you can bet your bottom dollar that he wouldn't stop until he'd tracked every last one down and taken them back. Graham did not like that idea, so he bypassed Maddox completely and gave the project to me alone. My orders were to sit on it; to protect the reservation and all information about it. Maddox was never to find out about the reservation. He tried when he took over from Graham; he sent missions all over the Rockies, Andes, the Himalayas looking for the missing bigfoots, skunk apes and nakannis."

"And?" pressed Ham.

"Maddox was retired for treading on too many peoples toes too often. He went private, hunting cryptids for foreign governments. After we ruined his little money-making scheme with the kelpies last year, he moved to plan B. Find the bigfoot family and sell to the highest bidder."

"You knew about the reservation, but you kept quiet about it. You knew that Maddox was not dead, but you failed to let us know."

"You kidnapped American citi… stole American property and didn't tell us." Slaughter countered.

"And Maddox?" Ham asked calmly, ignoring the reply.

"We only just found out, well, fairly recently. We thought Maddox had perished as well, but then we got word that he was putting together another team of mercenaries to go after the bigfoot and all its friends. At the moment they are wandering around the Nahanni National Park. His guide claims to be a Slavey of the Dene First nation, but is, in reality, a Naha. He is not only a Naha but a CSOR lieutenant in Ivor's team. He is, I believe, leading the good ex-colonel on a wild goose chase up and down the Mckenzie and Nahanni Rivers."

"We would have contacted you sooner, but General Maxwell had already contacted Ivor's boss and started to make arrangements for you to come across and save the day. My boss says that I am to work with you again. I have no problem with that. Do you?" Ham shook his head slowly.

"How did you know about my," waving a thumb at Kennedy, "our intentions.?"

"We have our ways colonel," Slaughter replied cryptically.

"So much for the Five Eyes[15]." Muttered Kennedy. Ham smirked. By unanimous unspoken agreement, they dropped the matter; there were more important matters on the table.

"Ham you are the senior officer, and if you don't mind me saying so, far more experienced, you take the lead, and we'll throw our teams in with you. Agreed Dave." Dave Slaughter agreed.

Ham stood up. "First, we need another mug of tea."

[15] Five countries, Australia, Canada, New Zealand, United Kingdom and United States form a joint espionage co-operation for signals intelligence. As well as listening to all other countries, some member states are not allowed to monitor their own citizens, so the others do and pass any relevant information back to that counties intelligence agencies.

Waddle like a Pregnant Penguin

After a quick stop at CFB Cold Lake on the flight from CFB Trenton to the Nahanni Valley, the passengers relaxed until the warning was given by the aircrew. Fifteen figures stood up and moved ungainly to the rear of the RCAF, Royal Canadian Air Force Lockheed Martin C-130J-30 Super-Hercules and prepared, checked and rechecked their equipment.

Wanting to insert themselves onto the DZ, drop zone covertly, the aircraft flew at eight thousand two hundred meters above sea level. The aircrew and passengers, human and animal, prepared to breathe oxygen. When the aircraft was about thirty kilometres away from the DZ, the crew and passengers went on oxygen and the aircraft decompressed. The rear doors were open. It was bitterly cold. The view through the rear doorway was white, with a little black and grey for contrast.

In the past, Ham had parachuted in various manners from aircraft, fixed-wing and rotor, by HAHO, HALO and static line, overall terrains imaginable from the desert, to the jungle, to mountainous snowfields. HAHOing onto a snowfield was his least favourite; difficult to see where you were going most of the time, and you never knew what lay beneath the snow on landing. He looked at each of the members of his team. The three SBS operators were acting nonchalant as if they did this every day. With the Canadian CSORs and Seals there, there was a lot of bravado on show. Macduff was doing her best to act like the rest, but Ham could see the slight look of uncertainty in her eye. Ham looked at her and knew she would jump without hesitation. Because of her size, Janet would jump in tandem with Captain Bouchard who was larger than Rob, the original choice. Just before they jumped, Janet strapped in front of Bouchard would lift her legs back out of the way so that he could support her weight and waddle to the door. John, carried Major, strapped to his front. Major wearing a special oxygen mask for dogs had done this before and displayed his casual bravado. Princess's head poked out of a warm bag strapped to Ham's chest, she wore an adapted small dog oxygen mask and seemed to be sulking. They all carried their rucksacks behind their legs. When they neared the ground, they would release the load so that it could dangle from a cord and not be in the way when they landed.

The others had all HAHO'd in training and on operations and stood patiently for the signal to go.

The loadie pointed to the signal lamp and shouted, "Red Light!" There was so much background noise that hardly anyone heard him. They followed the loadies hand signals.

The loadie pointed at the now, green light shouted and signalled for the jumpers to exit. Major Kennedy led the way, waddling the few steps onto the ramp and off the end into nothingness

Captain Bouchard and Janet followed as he had the heaviest load. The others followed quickly behind. There were no fancy exits; they just stepped off and out. Morello and Jaimie spun immediately to face back towards the aircraft, but that was their choice as they found that more convenient to stabilise themselves. Rob walked off the ramp with a nod to the aircrew, Ham followed.

Behind Ham, two cylinders with attached parachutes were released and pushed off the ramp.

Ham stabilised quickly, about fifteen meters out and pulled his 'D' ring. He felt the sudden jolt of the square type RAM parachutes deploying. It was always a good feeling when that happened. He looked up checked his rig and satisfied, checked that Princess was still secure and her oxygen mask was still in place. He looked around and checked that the two cylinders hung suspended beneath chutes not too far away. Ham guided his chute closer to the other jumpers. Where he went, the cylinders followed. All the parachutists and equipment came together and with everyone accounted for they headed off in the desired direction, guided by the GPS devices strapped to their forearms.

They flew their chutes north-west. Ham reckoned it would take about thirty-five to forty-five minutes to reach their destination, depending on the somewhat notorious winds in that area. They all followed their own path, but Kennedy, with his knowledge of the area, led the way.

Happy Landings

The landing was pretty uneventful, no broken necks or bones, not even a scratch. The equipment landed after and near Ham. The teams retrieved the contents and distributed the snowshoes and specialist weapons around the group.

Ham, Kennedy and Slaughter, confirmed their location and required direction of travel and followed Kennedy off the snowfield plateau to the north-west. Kennedy set the pace and rests.

Bouchard pulled a makeshift sledge made from one-half of one of the cylinders. In the sledge lay, Major and Princess mostly covered by blankets. Major had tried to walk but kept sinking into the snow. Princess did not even try.

Jaimie pulled the other half of the cylinder with some of the equipment packed in it. Rob relieved him at intervals. Morello offered to relieve Bouchard, but he shrugged her off, saying it was no hardship as the animals were light, so she shrugged and let him carry on.

Janet and Macduff had never walked in snowshoes before, but they soon found their rhythm.

Ham noticed that John always walked behind him. He had caught a look between Janet, Macduff and John and knew that John was keeping an eye on him by common agreement. He found it amusing.

They reached the lip of the Nahanni Valley before dark and set up camp in the tree line.

John insisted in setting up Ham's bivouac; Ham resisted for a short time then admitted defeat and let him get on with it. The fact was, Ham was more tired than he hated to admit. Sixty-two was not an age to be galivanting about in the snow-covered Canadian North-West Territories. The other two SBS operators helped Janet and Macduff set up their bivouacs. The SEALs set up theirs, and the Canadians wondered around the camp after building theirs, with critical eyes, as this was their area of expertise. There was a certain amount of quiet good-natured critiquing and ridiculing. With sentries posted, the rest prepared self-heating military rations in silence. Most of the soldiers and sailors had been in similar situations in Afghanistan. The last time Ham had prepared similar bivouac was when he had to resettle the Yetis to a more remote area in the Himalayas. That was many years ago. Ham had forgotten how many years ago that was.

In this hostile environment, you rest when you can; eat when you can, and most importantly, you replenish lost fluids whenever you can. Ham did not know about the others, but he knew he was sweating with the exertions. The operators heated snow and handed out hot drinks. Ham missed his tea. They knew they were not on a camping holiday; this was an operation, but Ham did think to go without his tea was very uncivilised.

Everything had gone so far as planned, so when Kennedy, Slaughter and Ham met for a council of war, it was agreed to follow the original plan. Each leader then went to his team and held an informal 'Chinese Parliament', where each had a say in the planning of the operation. Again, because everything was going according to plan, the meeting was short, and they crawled into their bivouacs to

sleep.

The Night Attack

Morello and Rob were out on sentry duty. Bouchard was out on roving picket duty. Ham had seen him go out, a huge bear-like creature loping off into the shadows of the trees.

Apart from a gentle breeze in the upper branches, the area was silent. Major slept soundly, with his head poking out of the sleeping bag, his ears moving to any sound. Of Princess, there was no sign apart from occasional movement deep in the footwell of the same sleeping bag.

Ham wondered if he had made the right decision coming on this operation, but he reasoned, to whom could he delegate? The other team leaders were more than competent, but he, Ham was the only one who had worked with the Naha and the bigfoot. Of course, the Naha Lieutenant Ataitcho, presently 'misguiding' Colonel Maddox's party knew the Naha and knew the bigfoot, but, he did not have enough seniority to command three teams of special forces operators. Tomorrow was another day and after a good night's sleep, Ham would feel refreshed. He pushed aside thoughts of the mission and tried to sleep.

His instinct or second sight warned him that something was wrong. He had not heard or smelt anything, but he knew that there was a presence. He opened his eyes to see Major and then Princess staring at him and then out into the dark. Major started to growl deep in his throat. Ham shushed him. Princess's hair stuck out, and she bared her teeth. Ham slowly and quietly got out of his bag and did his boot laces up. He climbed out of the bivouac and holding his machine pistol; he stared around. He noticed that Slaughter and Kennedy had also emerged. They saw him. He moved around the camp to wake Macduff and the SBS operators only to find them already awake. He let Janet sleep, although done with the best of intention, that might have been a mistake. They stood armed, alert and ready. They waited, searching. Those that had night vision devices attached to their helmets used them, while those that had them attached to their firearms used those, and those without stared into the darkness. Nothing moved, nothing made a sound.

If Ham had been alone, he might have imagined that he had made a mistake, but they were not all mistaken. There was something or someone out there, watching them

With a crash of branches and a roar, the creature rushed into the camp heading towards Janet's bivouac. They could not fire as to do so would be to invite friendly fire. Ham drew his knife and saw several of the young operators already rushing forward with their's drawn and ready. Janet awoke with a start and stared with horror at the oncoming creature. Another roar, more branches breaking, this time to the side, a shape larger than the bear burst from the trees and attacked with such force that both creatures flew away from Janet and into the darkness of the trees. Ham resheathed his knife and signalled for the others to hold back. Janet came and stood by Ham. She held his arm for comfort.

The battle was loud and vicious. They could hear the roars, the growls, the grunts, the breaking of branches, the cries, and then the silence. After a while, they heard one creature drag the other further into the forest. Then nothing.

Capt. Ettienne Bouchard did not eat breakfast the next day. Nothing was said to him about the night before.

Kennedy pulled Slaughter and Ham to one side.

"Bears are normally hibernating at this time of the year. Something or someone disturbed it enough for it to attack," he said. We should be very vigilant. The bear wanted to attack Janet. I can see that she is a cryptid, but why her?"

"She is a selkie, you know, sometimes seal and sometimes human. Maybe it wanted seal meat.?"

"Better tell my guys to watch it," quipped Slaughter the SEAL boss.

"I'd like a word with Bouchard. Then, I think a little Chinese Parliament is in order."

Kennedy sent Captain Bouchard over to report to Ham.

"Ettiene, when you disposed of the bear last night, were there any bullets in the meat?" Ettiene thought for a moment.

"To be honest, I don't know. When in the bear-dog form I don't exactly nibble delicately. Let me go and check the carcass; it is not far." Bouchard jogged off into the trees.

The rest of the men women and animals gathered around.

"We'll wait for Captain Bouchard; he's running an errand for me."

Bouchard returned shortly afterwards.

"Yes sir, there were, mostly 9mm. I wonder if I will get lead poisoning." He stated.

"Right, somebody shot that bear and I guess that the shooters were Maddox's hooligans. Ivor, while your Lieutenant Ataitcho is "misguiding" Maddox around the valleys, I reckon Maddox's either covering his bets and sending out at least one other team out searching; or he's on to Ataitcho and is trying to deceive us again. He is a sneaky bastard so that it could be either.

Ettiene, I want you to scout out in front and report back who's out there and what they're up doing. When Ettiene comes back, we'll reassess but my basic idea is that we ambush them and get them out of the way. Snipers to take out the leadership and radio operator, the rest of us to generally go and kick bottom."

"We have three sniper rifles, we're all qualified, who will be the snipers?" Ham looked at the two senior officers.

"Sam Wainwright is our best shot," suggested Slaughter.

"Toni Morello is ours," stated Kennedy.

"Rob, you up for it?" Rob nodded. "Ok, Rob Ingram is the third."

Bouchard raised a hand, Ham seeing it nodded to him. "Morello and I are the best snow workers. Sorry guys, you may be good at paddling in the sea, but this is our area of expertise. Make someone else the sniper, and we will go in, take out any sentries and reduce the opposition like white ghosts." There were a few chuckles. Ham nodded and looked around; there were no counter-suggestions.

"John, you take Morello's place. You're sniper three, agreed?" John nodded. "Ok Ettiene, when you are ready, off you go. We'll follow the same heading as yesterday, north-west. Report back if anything interesting, or even if blank. Until then, same as yesterday, two flankers, but not too far out. Anybody got any comments or suggestions? No? Ok, Ettiene, go off when you are ready and take care."

"Yes, boss." And he was gone. Ham saw Morello, retrieving his uniform from the bushes later. He had gone beast again. She did look after him, Ham thought.

They broke camp and continued their journey.

Surprise!

The snow was still falling lightly, most of it staying on the tree branches. Luckily breeze was still, the next gust of wind threatened to bring it all down. The temperature during the day was a steady bloody cold.

Ham trudged along, his mind full of plans and ideas. How on earth was he going to keep Maddox and his gang away from the nakanni? Once again, the general did not want prisoners. Ham decided it should depend on where the enemy ended up and what they had learned, there had after all been many hunts for the North American bigfoot, Scottish Nessie, American Chessie, Swedish Storsföodjuret. You couldn't go around killing all the hunters, even if the general thought you should.

It was getting darker, and they would soon have to stop for the night.

Suddenly and without warning, a dark, hairy, face full of teeth appeared in front of Ham. Ham fell back, his ankles caught in the snow. He snatched for his pistol, but it was deep in his clothing to stop it freezing. He pulled out his knife and saw John Patterson race past him towards the beast.

"Stop! John, stop!" he yelled. John came to a halt, he looked down at Ham and up at the beast. It was huge, larger than a bear, but muscular like a wolf. The beast stood on all fours, and the shoulders were at the same height as John's. The beast sat back and its large red tongue hung out of the side of its mouth dripping hot saliva onto the snow.

"Bloody Hell Bouchard, I nearly shat myself," Ham shouted at the bear-dog, "Can't you approach any other way?" If it were ever possible for a ferocious, deadly creature to look pitiful, Bouchard was doing his best. The beast hung its head and the eyes looked sad, it whimpered. Ham wondered what he was supposed to do; he was sorry that he had shouted in anger, pat it, stroke it?"

"He doesn't know any better when he is in this form," came an angry voice to the side. Ham looked up and saw Morello holding Bouchard's boots and clothes.

John helped Ham to his feet as the others approached.

"We'll take a break here until I get a chance to talk to Bouchard. Morello, give him his clothes please." Ham had expected Bouchard to wander off behind a bush to transform or he had a smooth transformation like Janet's, one-minute human, next minute seal and vice versa.

Bouchard looked at Ham; then he stared straight ahead focussing he growled deep in his throat, his bones creaked and cracked, his muscles tensed, snapped, shrunk, the hair, nails withdrew and sank back into his body, and he cried with pain, tears dripping from the anguished eyes. Ham had never seen anything like it. It took a few agonising minutes, but in the end, a naked Bouchard stood in front of them, exhausted. Morello stepped forward and gave him his clothes. Ham looked over at Janet who looked on disinterestedly. Macduff took in Bouchard's muscular physic and smiled when she realised that Ham was observing her interest.

Bouchard used the cloths to wipe away the sweat and then dressed quickly, like Janet when she was in seal form, he could withstand extreme cold, but as soon as they took on the human form, they were affected by the cold the same as humans.

Ham noticed that as Bouchard dressed in the many layers of clothing, he became... well, normal. Finished dressing, Bouchard stood calmly in front of the audience as if nothing had happened. Ham spoke to the gathering.

"Make some temporary shelters until I learn what the captain has to say. I think he could do with a hot drink; I know I could, tea please for me." The crowd dispersed. "Ivor, Dave, please stay." Ham called out. "Ask one of your team to sort out your shelters. Let's hear what he has to say."

Looking for Bear

"About ten clicks[16] north-west there is a group of about thirty men heading north. I guess that they are rank amateurs with little training, possibly paramilitaries or special forces wannabees. They have little tradecraft but all the gear, probably bought online in America or at gun shows. Their leader seems to have some skills, but no-body is listening to him. I'd reckon, he's someone from lower-tier[17] who wishes he made upper tier, Airborne at best. I left them settling in for the night, as I said all the best gear, but no idea how to use it. Campfires all over the place, you'd think they were going to roast wieners[18] and sing songs around the campfires for goodness sake. When I left, I didn't see any sentries. I think the leader told some guys to stand guard and they ignored him."

---

[16] Military slang or jargon for Kilometers

[17] In America Tier One is Delta Force, DEVGRU - SEAL Team Six, USAF Special Tactics Squadron and ISA Intelligence Support Activities (CIA), Tier Two is the rest of the SEAL Teams, Green Berets, Rangers, Marine Raiders and Force Recon, USAF Combat Controllers Tier Three is Airborne and specialist conventional forces, like 10 Mountain Division, Marine corps Recon Battalions. Navy Riverines etc

[18] Frankfurter / Vienna sausages

"Night vision capabilities?" Ham asked.

"Some of it is the best on the market, but I get the impression they don't know how to use it."

"Communications?"

"A couple of Sat phones. I saw some trying to get reception on mobile phones," Bouchard laughed.

"About thirty, you say?"

"It's difficult to say as they straggle out and wander off all over the place. I won't be surprised if some are lost further back on the trail."

"Good report, well done. Go and grab some food." Bouchard wondered off.

"What are your rules of engagement?" Ham asked the two senior officers. They looked at each other, then Slaughter spoke first.

"My boss says you decide. No restrictions. He knows that this is a blacker than black operation." He looked at Kennedy.

"Same here. We'll follow your lead. No need to point out that this is Canada, these guys are wandering around illegally armed and my guess is they will use those weapons at the earliest opportunity. They were never here as far as I'm concerned." Ham replied to them both.

"After what Bouchard said, we have a few choices; we can go in guns blazing and wipe them out to a man, leave no sign, end of the story. We could let them carry on; they're heading in the right direction, they'll find the Naha, or should I say, the Naha will find them, then you have a whole bunch of headless corpses, or option three, behind the blue door, we have, take them prisoner. But the last thing we want is thirty prisoners. I have an idea and it will involve both American and Canadian military co-operation."

"Well?"

"My country will probably go for it if you do eventually tell us your cunning plan."

"Gentlemen, gentlemen. This plan involves a lot of thought."

"I get it; I'll get someone to make you a cup of tea." Ham grinned.

By Strength and Guile

'By Strength and Guile' is the SBS motto. Ham's plan as discussed and agreed with Slaughter and Kennedy certainly needed a fair measure of both.

They broke camp a couple of hours after agreeing to the plan. They left in two groups, The snipers, Morello and Bouchard in the first and the rest following in the second with the equipment. It was dark but the moonlight was bright enough to allow a steady pace without the need for night vision equipment.

It took the snipers about two hours to cover the undulating landscape to Maddox's men's camp. They crept in the last kilometre until they were so close they could have shot the ears off the leaders as he slept. Bouchard and Morello scouted the perimeter and found no sentries. They went round again as they could not believe it the first time. Nobody was that amateurish.

Bouchard left to guide in the main group. The Canadian, American and British special forces operators moved into position.

Ham held back with Macduff, Janet and the animals. They had agreed time and synchronised watches, everybody waited.

As the minute struck, Bouchard and Morello moved in. They crept forward in the snow, avoiding winter dried branches and crackable ice. Behind them, the others followed as carefully.

Morello was the first to reach one of Maddox's party, a hand over his mouth and a knife against his throat was enough to ensure compliance. He put his hands behind his back as quietly but firmly ordered. A rag in his mouth and his wrists then feet tied with a cord was enough to incapacitate him. Another strip of rag tied the gag in place. A gentle word of warning with the knife tickling his neck enough to draw a little blood was more than enough.

Bouchard's victim started to struggle, so the fellow found himself unconscious and trust up like a chicken ready for the oven. The rest of the teams moved in; each victim had a choice, conscious or unconscious. The response was fifty-fifty in the end. The operators did not mind. Not a word above a whisper spoken. The operators checked the number and found one short. They rechecked, but still no joy.

He found them, he had been relieving himself in the forest and returned to a dimly lit camp, full of tied up bodies, his comrades and some dark, mysterious figures. He turned to run, dropping his expensive rifle. He got two steps before Major brought him down. His screams were the only loud sounds that night. Jaimie fed up with the irritating noise, knocked him unconscious and called Major off. Major had not had this much fun in ages and was, therefore, a bit reluctant, but he did obey, wanting the man to move again. Princes and Ham walked over and looked at the last captive as Jaimie trussed him up.

Ham looked at Princess, who had suddenly become agitated, staring down the path south. Moments later, Major reacted, from a sitting start, he was off as fast as his four feet could carry him. John went after him, toe feet being not quite as fast, but he did put on a good turn of speed.

A few moments later, there was a blood-curdling scream, a growl and another cry. The others waited. A few minutes later, John returned dragging the unconscious body of a straggler from Maddox's group along behind him. Major proudly trotted along behind with a piece of material as a trophy in his mouth. John threw him down and Jamie tied him up like the rest.

Ham sent John and Major back on the trail in case there were other stragglers. Then they waited for dawn. Ham muttered something about being thirst, and a mug of tea magically appeared a short while later.

Ham sat with Slaughter and Kennedy and reviewed their plan. So far, everything had gone better than expected; none saw a need to amend the plan.

Sign Sealed and Delivered

Ham stood off to the side in the shadows; this was not his play. Princess sat on a log nearby watching the spectacle.

All the operators stood in front of the row of mercenaries whose wrist and feet restraints roughly removed. A little blood had spilt in the process, was part of the plan. Macduff, Janet and Morello stood with the operators, their lower face also covered by a scarf, but obviously and deliberately still looking like women. Bouchard, as planned, was the only operator not present.

Kennedy took the lead, standing in front of the teams, casually holding a PGW Defence Technologies Inc. C14 Timberwolf MRSWS[19] sniper rifle across his chest. It was a statement; we hold power over you, do not mess with us.

"Gentlemen," he started calmly. "you have entered Canadian sovereign territory armed for war. I don't like that. Who the Hell do

---

[19] Medium Range Sniper Weapon System

you think you are committing this act of war?" The leader looked as if he was about to speak."

"Shaddap! You asshole!" shouted Slaughter in as rough an American accent as he could imagine. "You don't fight for America! And yet you come here armed to attack our allies. You must be terrorists!" Again, the leader wanted to speak. "I said shaddap!"

Kennedy could see by the look in their eyes that they were ready for stage two. "Strip!"

Nobody moved. Every operator and the ladies raised their weapons.

"Are you deaf I said strip. Everything off right now!"

"You're gonna kill us," whined one of the men.

"We will if you do not strip, now," Kennedy said with an evil grin on his face. First one and then the rest stripped down to their underpants. "Everything!" A few seconds later, the row of men stood on the snow holding their freezing testicles stared at Kennedy and the women."

CPO Apps and Jaimie collected all the webbing, belts, shirts, underclothes. John and CPO Wainwright collected the contents of their pockets. Morello checked the remaining articles for hidden weapons, as she did so, she looked tutted and laughed at the men's shrunken embarrassment. The three girls pointed and giggled as instructed, increasing the captive's unease. The British military play similar games with the special forces at DSTO[20] at RAF St Mawgan called SERE[21]. All the operators had gone through something similar. These amateurs did not know what hit them.

"You can't do this…" He stopped as Slaughter slowly lowered the rifle and pointed it at him.

"I told you twice. I will not tell you again. Capice?[22]" The terrified nod in reply showed that he understood.

"Get dressed in your boots, socks, trousers, jackets and hat, nothing else!" barked Kennedy. He waited until they had sullenly did so. Some were smart enough to realise that if they were being

---

[20] Defense Survival Training Organisation
[21] Survive, Evade, Resist, Extract
[22] Italian phrase commonly used in America – Understand?

allowed to dress, chances were that they would not end up shot. Kennedy continued, "Some of you will have met our American military war dog; I would like to introduce you to our Canadian military war dog. Before I do, I must warn you to remain still." The men were puzzled. They became frightened when the growling started behind them. It was deep and loud. They did not move, but their eyes tried to see behind them. Slowly the growling got louder. They could hear the footsteps behind as the growls moved along the line behind them. The operators looked on with bored looks on their faces.

Bouchard came to the last man and turned the corner.

"Holy shit!" exclaimed the man at the end. The rest turned their heads and looked. Various expletives followed. Fear covered their faces as the bear-dog walked slowly along the line, eyeing each man in turn. Reaching the end of the line; the beast walked slowly back into the forest, growling and snarling as he did so. Ham thought it was a marvellous performance; nobody would believe a word of their story.

"You will be taken for a short walk. There will only be a couple of men guarding you, but Fang will be there, following you, watching you. If you try to escape the guards have orders to shoot to kill if you survive Fang. Am I understood?" He was understood.

"Johnson, give them their rations and lead them off." Lt. Joe Pottkamp, alias Johnson, called them forward and Rob gave each enough rations for one meal.

"Where are we going?" was followed by a phut as a suppressed shot kicked up a clump on snow between the leader's feet. He yelped and jumped.

When each man had his rations, Pottkamp and Wainwright, alias Thompson, led the captives off. Bouchard made an occasional growl or fleeting appearance to keep the men in order. Pottkamp and Wainwright could have guided the men without weapons, they were not going anywhere. After a cold night just inside the furthest treeline near to where Ham had camped the first night, the men escorted to the original landing zone.

Wainwright gave four men spades, which frightened them, as they thought they were supposed to dig their own graves. Pottkamp ignored their pleas and made them dig where the SEALS had buried their expensive parachutes. Shortly after they had retrieved the chutes, two aeroplanes arrived and hovered nearby. They were V-22 tiltrotor Ospreys. Pottkamp knew that an HC-130 Hercules capable of refuelling these aircraft was circling somewhere above, ready for the return journey to California. The Ospreys landed and Pottkamp went over and talked to the crews. He came back with four Marine Corps Police Officers, two from each aircraft. He separated the men and gave them to the military police officers. The marines covered the men, barked orders and made it clear that they were not in the mood for any trouble.

The Ospreys took off vertically and started to angle off for horizontal flight south.

Pottkamp and Wainwright returned to the others.

Deception

Ham had made camp about twenty kilometres up the Headless Valley from their previous location, in the Nahanni Nation Park Reserve as everyone agreed the site chosen by the weekend warriors was abysmal from a military point of view. He let the operators choose the site once he had selected the area, but he could see straight away why they had chosen it, the position was defensible and practical. From there, they could see up and down the valley while not being seen. He left the construction of the temporary shelters and defences to the fitter younger men and women. Even Janet joined in with the manual labour and she was over two hundred years old.

Ham did not sit around wasting time; however, asking John to accompany him, he walked and scrambled with Major and Princess, exploring the environment. It had been a long time since he had been in this area and he needed to re-orientate, the place he sought was somewhere in the mountains between the third and second canyon in the Headless Range He knew the entrance to the Naha land was nearby, he just had to remember where. He reminded John that he did not want to be surprised by the Naha, as he had too much respect for his head and he wanted it to remain stuck on his head. They may not remember him. He hoped so because he had that itch that told him that he was under observation.

The two SEALs and Bouchard who had accompanied the prisoners, returned to the fold several days later. They had followed the valley north-west along the South Nahanni River until they reached the Headless Valley. Here they reported to Ham.

As instructed, Bouchard had kept his distance, but had made his presence felt, Lt. Joe Pottkamp had remained cold and aloof, while CPO Sam Wainwright had been approachable when Pottkamp was elsewhere. The prisoners seeking solace in their predicament had spoken freely to him.

"Maddox is further east down the South Nahanni River. He has about twenty men with him. They are more hardcore, a mixture of ex-special forces from different lands, a right old mixture by all accounts, Russian Spetznaz, SAS, Eastern Block, Western, Asian, ex-French Foreign Legion; you name it. I don't know if he sent the ones we got as bait, but he certainly kept the 'A' team with him. Ataitcho is still his not too efficient guide, but Maddox is getting impatient. The leader said they used to report in twice a day, so we can assume that Maddox is heading to their last known location. We saw no sign of them yet." Pottkamp reported.

"Good, well done. Anything else?" Ham looked at the men and the bear-dog Bouchard. He had to restrain himself from patting him on the head, 'Good Boy'.

"What's going to happen to those prisoners?" Wainwright asked.

"I'll leave that up to your boss. I think they should enjoy the inside of a military prison, at least until this show is over, threatened with Guantanamo Bay, then told they would be on an official watch list for terrorists, but released."

"What if they talk, sir?"

"Who's going to believe them? By the time they tell the story, we would become a hundred with Super-Special Forces and dozens of large ferocious Canadian war dogs as big as cars. No, they'll become the joke they are."

"Go and have something to eat and drink and settle in, again, Good job. Etienne, can you stay for a moment?" The others walked off. Morello appeared with Bouchard's clothes. Ham pointed to a rock a short distance away. She took the hint and left. "Ettiene, I saw what you go through to change, so I want you to hear me out before you 'change'," Bouchard grunted. "I know that the entrance to the Naha land is in the mountains nearby. I want to find it before Maddox gets here. I can describe it to you and give you a sketch, but I need you in the bear-dog form to look for it. You can change and change back later, or you can stay as you are, it's up to you. I don't want to cause you any more hurt than is necessary." The bear-dog snorted and walked over to his clothes, where he went through the agonies of the transformation. When the change was complete, he dried himself, dressed and reported back to Ham.

"It is not as bad as it seems colonel," he said calmly, "the body produces hormones like endorphins which ease the process," he grinned, "a bit like a woman giving birth."

"I'll take your word for that."

"This place you want me to look for colonel?" Ham took out a notepad and pencil; he drew as he talked. Afterwards, Ham shook his hand; he had decided not to pat him on the head.

Disappearance

Ham sat on his new favourite rock looking at the camp below. Bouchard had eaten, drunk some coffee and disappeared back into the forest. Janet had taken Major for a walk, and Macduff was helping the others sort out defences, bivouacs and bashas[23] for the equipment, all of which, had to blend into the countryside. The sentries were out. It was the quiet before the storm, the time when Ham thought, planned and rethought his options.

He had just begun to hear a noise when a hand covered his mouth and pulled him back. His arms pinioned behind him; Ham was carried away. He struggled to free himself and received a blow to the head for his troubles. He fell into darkness.

He did not know how long he had been out for the count, but it was dark, then he realised that he was blindfolded, arms and legs were also tied. He shook his head to try to clear it of the throbbing headache; it did not help; it made it worse, his head swam in the

---

[23] A low-lying British Military waterproof cover for people or equipment, normally a camouflaged sheet strung between two trees with paracod.

darkness. He could not see but he could hear someone or something moving around. He moved his head to try to locate the sound. Yes, they were footsteps; it was a person walking slowly. He heard more people moving around, quicker, possibly younger, certainly lighter on their feet. He had no gag, so he spoke.

"Where am I? Who are you?" he asked knowing that the questions might not receive an answer, but any answer might give him a clue, an accent, the wording, the tone, something, anything. There was no reply, but the person or people walking stopped, so he tried again.

"Who are you? Why am I here?" There was silence. After a while, there was a child-like chuckle.

"How good is your memory Captain Hamilton? Hmmm?" Ham dug into his mind and at the same time tried to work out who it could be logically. It was a voice from his past, a long distant past.

"Shaman Drygeese?"

"Yessss. Shaman Drygeese. You said you would not return Captain Hamilton, why do you break your word?" Ham felt the prick of the knife against his throat. "Why do you bring men and women here? Why do you bring the bear-dog here? You bring a dog with metal teeth? Metal teeth, weren't his original teeth good enough? Why you bring a cat? A cat! What good is a cat?" Something was wrong here; Ham could hear a cat purring.

"Shaman Drygeese, are you playing with my cat?"

"We are talking." the Shaman laughed, and the blindfold was whipped away from Ham's face. In front of him sat a very old wrinkled face crone, most of her teeth were missing, which became obvious when she smiled, and she was smiling at Ham. "Cut him loose," she instructed in English, a young Naha boy dressed in buckskins complied. "He is my apprentice, very skilled, maybe better than you one day, boundary walker." She spoke again to the boy in Naha, a variation of the Athabaskan or Dene language and he left the room. He returned shortly afterwards with a hot liquid which had obviously been cooking next door; he presented the drink to Ham. "It is not the tea, you devour so readily Captain Hamilton, but it is good for you." Ham drank it slowly; it was pleasant, not too bad.

"Why am I here like this? Why kidnap me? I would come to your campfire gladly."

"You bring men and guns, not to mention the bear-dog? Were you expecting an invitation? The younger warriors wanted to remove your heads from your shoulders, luckily the elders intervened. They thought I should talk to you first; you may still end up with nowhere to place your hat." She giggled at her little joke. Ham wondered how much was a joke, the Naha of the not too distant past were head-hunters.

"The men and women outside are here under my command, and the command of the leaders of the land outside to protect you, the nakanni and the other creatures I brought here for you to revere and protect." She looked at him with her cloudy grey eyes surrounded by wrinkles on wrinkles on wrinkles. It was difficult to know what she was thinking.

He continued, "Shaman Drygeese, you know I have the second sight, two men in the group also have the gift, a woman has it, but she is not yet trained. The two men, one from Canada and one from America, are leaders of teams of warriors sent to protect the nakanni and the other creatures. The woman I am training when I pass over, she will take my place. The bear-dog is a were-animal; he can be human or beast. He is a warrior of Canada. There is a woman who can change from seal to woman at will; she is also on my team. The dog is my guardian; he for my protection, so was the cat."

"This cat protects you," she laughed, stroking the purring Princess.

"She has her ways," he replied. "The rest are warriors, we trust. They fight to protect the nakanni and any other creature that needs our help." Ham wondered why he was explaining so much. He felt he did not want to but could not help himself. Shaman Drygeese creased her wrinkles into a smile at his confusion.

"The drink helps loosen your tongue, Captain Hamilton. You want to talk, and you want to tell me the truth. You may walk away with your head held high yet, or someone else might." He thought she smiled at him, but with all the wrinkles, it was difficult to say. "One of our people is coming here. He brings many men, warriors; this leader is a bad man."

"This man is my enemy; he comes to take the nakanni, the bigfoot and the others away. Other people will pay him money and he will sell the nakanni to them. The Naha, Ataitcho that walks with him works for us, he has been trying to lead them away, but now he brings them to us and we will kill this man Maddox and his men to protect the Naha secret." She started to stand. He wanted to help her, but she waved him back down.

"I will go and talk to the Grandfather of our tribe about this. Piqtoukun will give you another drink; it is safe. This one will stop you telling me all your secrets, or you might tell me your true thoughts about your dead friend's wife, Janet." She giggled as she finally stood up and hobbled away still chuckling. Ham sat there stunned, what did she mean and how on earth could she know about Jack and Janet Drummond?

The Grandfather

A warrior dressed in tanned skins and moccasin boots walked into the cave, he waved at Ham to follow him. The warrior led the way, not checking whether Ham followed him or not. Of course, he would.

The tunnel was wide and high, lit by flaming torches that had blackened the walls and ceilings over many decades or centuries. They walked through a cavern, another tunnel, they followed some steps down and up and around corners, taking left turns and right turns. Ham lost his sense of direction and gave up trying to remember where they had been. He noticed that the corridors became warmer and loosed his jacket. He could feel the sweat trickle down his back.

Suddenly they came into the opening of a large canyon with tall irregular cantilevered walls. The sky ran like an upside-down winding river between the closing edges of the walls disappearing into the distance. There was daylight. The light shone down in a ragged sheet over the green forest of ferns, wild cherry and fruit trees. A river meandered through the canyon, spotted with hot steam rising from occasional hot spring pools. He had not seen it for over forty years but it was as Ham remembered it, beautiful. Birds flew lazily through the canyon, under the overhanging rock. They could fly away, but why should they fly into the snow and blizzards above the gap. Ham spotted wildlife in the trees, glades and by the riverbanks. He spotted a couple of young bigfoot playing under a tall Oaktree. It was tall and old, but the size of the cavern dwarfed it.

The warrior tapped Ham's arm and walked on. They came to a clearing and there on a large felled tree sat an old man., near but behind the old man sat an old woman. Their dress was plain old, worn, but comfortable looking patterned pale buckskins. Shaman Drygeese sat on a patterned woven rug laid on the grass nearby. Ham walked up and stood in front of the Grandfather. Something tingled in Ham's mind. The Grandfather looked at him sternly. The thought grew, he discarded it. The old woman behind the grandfather sat smiling at him. There was something, it formed again and he was about to ignore it when he suddenly discovered the truth.

"Abercrombie!" he exclaimed. The Grandfather burst into laughter. The old woman giggled. Shaman Drygeese rubbed her hands in delight. "Corporal Simon Abercrombie of the Royal Canadian Mounted Police, what on earth are you doing here? We left in nineteen seventy-five."

"Seventy-six," corrected the old man. Then Ham realised, Abercrombie was not old, they were both old. If anything, Abercrombie was slightly younger. Long gone was his head of curly golden hair, replaced now with long straight silver and white hair held in place by a patterned beaded headband.

"As you can see, I am the Grandfather of the Naha tribe. You remember my wife, Chilam?"

"Now I remember, you were lovestruck on a small First Nation girl when we brought the bigfoot here. Jack Drummond dragged you off, but you kept professing your love to that young girl, what was she nineteen, twenty at the time?"

"Twenty-one and as pretty as they came." He turned and smiled at her. "Still is." Chilam smiled coyly. "When we finished the mission, I resigned and came back. The entrance was well hidden, but when they saw that I would not give up looking, they let me in. Initially, they wanted to kill me, but Chilam intervened, a real-life Pocahontas," he chuckled. "I eventually became part of the tribe. They were wary of me initially, a few warriors still wanted to part my head from my shoulders, but eventually, they accepted me. Over time I became an Elder and somehow they chose me to be the Grandfather. They chose me because they regarded me as wise and smart, can you believe that, me? And now, you stand in front of me Captain Hamilton, and I must pass judgement on you. I must decide what is good for the tribe." His face had become serious.

"Am I allowed to speak?"

"I assume you will anyway, go on."

"I brought warriors from the UK, USA and Canada to protect your tribe and the creatures here. They are all highly trained and specialists not only in fighting but in protecting creatures such as the nakanni. They will kill to protect the creatures."

"Why do you treat me like a fool Hamilton? Why do you call them warriors, do you think I do not remember soldiers and commandos?"

"The soldiers from Canada are part of CSOR, Canadian Special Operations Regiment; the Americans are SEALs, Sea Air and Land, they are sailors, the men from the UK are SBS, Special Boat Service operators. I call them warriors because they are, but these organisations did not exist when you came back here." The Grandfather looked thoughtful but appeared to accept the explanation.

"The beast, the bear-dog? Why did you bring him?'

"He is one of the Canadian party."

"The seal woman?"

"She is part of my team. She was Jack Drummond's wife. He died last year." The Grandfather nodded. "Shaman Drygeese tells me you have feelings for this woman."

"No! She was Jack Drummonds wife. You don't have feelings for your late friend's wife."

"What planet do you come from?" asked Abercrombie, shaking his head.

"These other men, why do you want to bring them here, then kill them? Why not kill them elsewhere?"

"One of your tribe, Ataitcho, has been trying to mislead them away from here, but they will get here eventually. They are determined. We need to close this matter once and for all."

"Maybe they would not come here if you had not captured those other men and taken them away? Maybe if you had left them alone, they would not know we are here?"

"That is a lot of maybes. They are getting too close. What if they had found the entrance?"

"We would kill them, rip off their heads," shrugged the Grandfather.

"You can't do that. You decapitate twenty men and the Canadian government would have to act. They would be swarming all over these mountains; you know that. Secondly, Maddox, you remember him, he was in the old American team, the one we had to avoid, he is the leader of these men. He is no longer working for the Americans; he has gone rogue. He would know where to look for you."

"He does now, thanks to you."

"My men will ambush and kill him and his men."

"And the government won't mind? How come it's ok for you, but not for my tribe?"

"Because we work for the government."

"Here, I am the government; we are the Nation. My men could kill you and your men, Maddox and his men and dump the headless bodies many mountains and valleys away from here." He opened his arms palms up. "And life in the valley goes on, and we live happily ever after."

"Why don't you let my men deal with them?"

"Why are you always wanting to kill Hamilton? Why kill these men and not the others?"

"Because these men are warriors and the others are not. We capture these men and take them away, as a matter of pride, they will return, and return, and keep returning." The Grandfather seemed to be considering the problem.

"The beast is coming. We eat. If the beast attacks any of my tribe or any of the creatures, we eat him," he started to rise.

"He comes to protect me, let me wait for him." The Grandfather looked across at the Shaman who gave a slight nod. The Grandfather sat down again and stared at the cave entrance behind Ham. Ham turned and stared too.

Beauty and the Beast

Like a dog released from the back of a car in a park, Bouchard bound out of the cave and came to a skidding halt. He was panting, his tongue flopping out his mouth. The sunlight temporarily blinded him. He looked around and saw Ham. Ham stood and opened his arms as if in supplication and the bear-dog came wearily forward. It had been a long search. Ham did something he thought he would never do, he patted and stroked Bouchard's head, but it seemed to work. Bouchard sat and looked at Ham and the others.

"He may change, and we will bring him clothes to fit his size," the Shaman stated. Bouchard looked at Ham, who nodded. Bouchard transformed with all the agonising growls, grunts and groans that always seemed to be part of the process. As he did, the birds flew away in alarm and the nearby young bigfoot cowered behind a tree. Standing naked covered in sweat, Bouchard faced Ham and the Nahas.

A few moments later, three young Naha maidens brought clothing for Bouchard. They smiled and giggled. Bouchard, sheepishly, dried himself from the sweat and dressed. The Naha maidens were shooed away by Shaman Drygeese. Either the Naha, did not think Ham knew what was going on, or they did not care, either way, he saw their machinations. Abercrombie slowly stood and with a flick of his wrist indicated for the others to follow. Chilam stood and followed a step or so behind the Grandfather.

Shaman Drygeese, waited for Ham to catch up before falling into step with him. Her slow hobble had disappeared, Ham wondered how much of it was affected. Bouchard brought up the rear, staring around at this oasis in the winter wilderness outside.

They walked to a large cave where thick woven rugs lay on the floor and furs stacked against the walls. The Grandfather sat, helped by his wife. The Shaman took her place and indicated where Ham and Bouchard should sit. The same maidens as before brought platters of meats, beans, cooked vegetables, fruit and cornbread. The Grandfather took a little and signalled the others to partake. The meat was tender venison pieces cooked in a tomato-based sauce. The meal was simple and filling. Princess who had stayed with the Shaman nibbled on the scraps she fed her. A cloudy cider which reminded Ham of Scrumpy accompanied the meal. Nobody talked during the meal. Ham looked around; it was in a similar cave that Ham had met the previous Grandfather of the tribe, Animiki. Animiki had been a strong, powerful man with a wicked sense of humour. Overjoyed with the addition of the bigfoots, stink-apes and yellow-tops, he, Jack and Ham had become great friends. Ham remembered now that Animiki had been very friendly with Abercrombie. Had he been planting the seed in Abercrombie's mind, that he should return? Was Abercrombie playing the same game with Bouchard?

The Grandfather hardly ate. His wife fussed over him. He smiled and shooed her away.

Ham looked at Abercrombie, the tribe's Grandfather did not have long to live, six months tops. Both the Grandfather and the Shaman saw his gaze.

"Shaman Drygeese, says seven months, what do you reckon Captain Hamilton?" Ham nodded and looked down. "There are some things that even Shaman Drygeese cannot fix," laughed the Grandfather. "We have another Grandfather in training lined up. I will introduce you to him later. The tribe will continue after my passing. What we need to discuss is the present."

The Shaman suddenly got up and hurriedly walked over to the Grandfather and whispered in his ear. He turned and whispered back to her. She nodded and left. The Grandfather seemed disturbed.

"Some more of your people come. The dog found the entrance; he probably followed the bear-dog. I do not like so many people knowing the secret of our nation."

"Who is coming?" Ham asked.

"The dog and two women, the seal woman and the one with the gift that she ignores."

"No-one else?"

"They come alone," stated Abercrombie.

"It is good that they are alone. The seal woman has kept her secret for hundreds of years, and I trust her completely. The other is my mentee; if you allow her to come here and learn, she will help protect your nation from the outside."

The Grandfather humphed and sat deep in thought for a while. Ham waited; it was all he could do.

"Why did you bring the seal-woman here? Is it because of your feelings for her?"

"No!" replied Ham with alacrity, "there are many lakes and rivers here. I did not know if we would need her skills in the water." The Grandfather humphed again.

"I still think it is because you have emotions for her." It was Ham's turn to humph. Ham looked at Abercrombie and thought that he saw a hint of a smile in his eyes.

A warrior escorted the two women and Major to the cave. Major walked calmly over and sat down beside Ham. His tail said that he was glad to be there. The Grandfather signalled that the ladies should sit near Ham. Janet sat on the side opposite Major and gently touched Ham's arm as she sat down. This act was not missed by Abercrombie, who looked at Ham with a, I told you so smile. Macduff sat beside Major. Princess left the Shaman and lay down between Major's paws. This act was also not missed by the Shaman who slowly nodded her head.

"Are we expecting anyone else?" the Grandfather asked in a tone that could only be construed as sarcastic. Ham looked at the ladies in turn, who shook their heads.

Ham introduced, Abercrombie, Chilam and Shaman Drygeese to his companions.

"Why are you here?" the Grandfather asked Macduff directly.

"We came to find Colonel Hamilton," she replied simply. Abercrombie nodded.

"Colonel, eh? You made colonel." Abercrombie pursed his lips and smiled at Ham. Ham did not reply.

"Why did you come here, Mrs. Drummond?" the Grandfather asked Janet. Janet seemed a little taken aback that he knew her name, but she quickly recovered.

"We all came looking for Colonel Hamilton." The Grandfather looked at Major. Major looked back at him and yawned disinterestedly.

"He does have metal teeth, wow! That is new to me. Why did you give him metal teeth?" Abercrombie looked at Ham puzzled.

"I didn't, the military did. The dog was badly injured in Afghanistan protecting his handler. The military honoured its bravery and rebuilt his jaw." The Grandfather looked at Major and smiled.

"We too admire bravery and loyalty." He paused for a while, as if deep in thought. "So what is it you want Colonel Hamilton? Think before you answer." Ham thought.

"I want to protect your people, this place, and the creatures that live here. I also want to eliminate Maddox the leader, for what he has done to other creatures, what he wants to do here and for what he will do in the future. The man is evil."

"So, you want to kill them all, that is a lot of men and a lot of killing. Is this the only solution? Would you consider other solutions?"

"Of course." Replied the curious Ham.

Another Solution

Ham and his companions returned to the camp, where the other special forces teams greeted them. They took in Bouchard's First Nation buckskin attire but did not ask any questions. Bouchard changed with thanks into the uniform brought to him by Sergeant Morello.

The three leaders moved to one side for a quiet chat at the place where Ham had been kidnapped. He looked behind where he had sat before and saw no sign of disturbance or footprints of his abductors. They all sat down.

"I have met with the Naha's, and we have agreed on a plan of action." The other two listened attentively. "It is a joint operation and we play the bait." Slaughter and Kennedy looked at each other and back to Ham. "We gentlemen are the 'B' team in this play. In a moment, I will explain the full plan, but I need you to understand, and then emphasise to your teams that the rules of engagement have just changed. Let me explain," and he did. When he finished, they discussed details. When they were satisfied, they agreed that the whole group, apart from sentries, hold a Chinese Parliament. Bouchard and Macduff would take over from the present sentries as they had already heard the plan that Ham agreed with the Grandfather.

The Chinese Parliament was kept brief, but included various, questions, suggestions and comments injected by nearly everyone. The result was more or less the same, but with a few tweaks. Ham was satisfied and closed the meeting. They dispersed to recheck their defensive positions.

Before dark, Bouchard changed and left the camp. They were not expecting visitors until the next day, but sentries were maintained, and everyone was teamed up in pairs or threes throughout the night, with one staying awake, while the other or others slept.

In the small hours, about two o'clock, there was gunfire and explosions somewhere in the distant valleys. This disturbance was according to plan, Bouchard was drawing them into their valley.

Bouchard returned about six in the morning. He was bleeding from an arm wound, but gently brushed off Morello's attempts at first aid. He changed and when he was human, the wound was gone. They had not used silver bullets.

"There are about fifty in all now. They are following me; Lord knows I left enough tracks, the blood was a touch of genius I thought, self-inflicted of course, they couldn't hit a barn door." Morello who was on the edge of the conversation, humphed in disgust, having wasted her sympathy. "If they can track through the night, they would be here about nineish, but if they wait until daylight to start, I reckon on about twelvish. I took my time getting here as I didn't want it to appear too obvious, but at the same time, I didn't want the poor devils to get lost." In the end, Maddox and his men appeared deep down at the mouth of the valley at eleven, give or take an 'ish'.

Each side knew the other's capabilities, the hunters wanting to track and attack, but they had no intention of walking into an ambush. As they came up the valley, they moved more cautiously.

The defenders watching their approach pretending to appear unaware of the mercenaries' approach, without appearing to do so, a glint of something shiny, a movement where there should not be, a pebble falling down the slope. It was against the grain for the teams to make these rookie mistakes, but little ones had to be put on, for the audience, not too much, just enough to tantalise and entice.

Those that had binoculars, view the spectacle below from shaded glasses. They could make out a portly leader, who they assumed was Maddox directing the much fitter looking hunters. Two teams were sent out to flank their position, sniper teams, shooters and spotters were sent out. Maddox was closing the trap.

The youth, who had assisted Shaman Drygeese, appeared at Ham's side. He had not heard or seen him until he was there.

"Three taken already," was all he said before he turned and disappeared into the undergrowth. Ham marvelled at his skill.

The boy kept reappearing every so often with a running total. Ham wondered if Maddox realised that his little army of mercenaries was dwindling by the minute.

Ham's group monitored the action from their positions, but they could not see what was happening or how it was happening. These special forces operators were experts in observing, but they saw nothing. All they saw was fewer and fewer hunters moving forward, the flank attackers had completely disappeared, and they could see no sign of the snipers and their spotters. The pine trees and undergrowth in the gaps were thick and Ham could only glimpse Maddox's progress every so often. The boy kept reappearing, this many now, now this many.

At one point, Maddox stopped and seemed to be staring around, Ham stood and ran in a stooped fashion that was sure to be seen, to another position. Maddox took the bait and signalled to those near him to proceed up the densely wooded mountain slope. They climbed the incline. Maddox was not young, about the same age as Ham, as he climbed, he focused more and more on the ground in front of him, failing to look around. Pausing, Maddox looked and then stared around. He could only see a few, maybe five of his men. Ham could not hear, but he could see Maddox gesturing, asking his men where the others were. They suddenly realised that they were alone. One of the hunters appeared to panic and fired up at the defensive position; he received a headshot in return. The others went to ground.

The boy reappeared to confirm the account, One dead, three plus the leader remain, the rest captured by the Naha.

Everyone waited to see what Maddox would do next; withdrawal was the answer. He brought his men closer to protect himself, as at heart he was always a coward, he was willing to attack with other men, who he was willing to sacrifice, or attack with overpowering forces, he was weak, a bully. Somehow the odds had turned against him and all he could think of was saving his skin.

Shaman Drygeese appeared beside Ham. Within a short while, she was fed the final running total by her assistant, four, three, two and then finally, Maddox.

Ham asked the Shaman if she was sure that all the men had been captured, the look she gave him, made him wish he had not asked.

When he asked about Maddox's Canadian special forces Naha guide, she just said it was all in hand.

While the others stayed in camp or on sentry duty, just in case, the Shaman took Bouchard, Janet, Macduff and Ham back to the cave entrance. Princess was in Ham's jacket breast, and Major followed Ham without being asked. She did not attempt to hide the entrance.

The Truth of Bigfoot

Shaman Drygeese led them through the labyrinth of tunnels and caverns to the land of the Naha and on to the Grandfather's cave. He was sat in the same place with Chilam sat to the side and slightly back. The Grandfather signalled them to be seated as before.

"So Colonel Hamilton, we have done more or less what we set out to do. We have captured all, but one of the mercenaries, one foolish fellow who decided to shoot it out. One of your men sent him to whichever heaven he believed. A pity, but inevitable." The grandfather looked at Ham and waited a few moments before he carried on. "So what do we do now, rip off their heads in good old Naha fashion, leave the bodies as a warning to others?" He shook his head and continued, "we did, we could, but we don't. Not for a hundred years. I will tell you what we are going to do, ready, listening?" Ham was feeling a little irritated, but he could see Abercrombie was having his fun. Ham waited and hid his impatience. "Shaman Drygeese, will give them a potion that will eradicate this whole episode from their minds for good, forever. When they recover, they will not remember a thing. Whatever they did before, no problem still there, but when she tells them not to remember anything about their expedition to the Makenzie Mountains and the Nahanni Nature Park Reserve and wherever else they have been while up here, gone." Ham began to understand the final part of the Grandfather's plan.

"And then what? Leave them wandering around outside?"

"No, no, nothing so cruel and inhumane, we will take them to different town and villages, without their weapons and other specialist equipment that your average person should not have and dump them on the outskirts. After that, what they do is up to them. They won't remember this place or anything that happened here."

"And Maddox?" Ham asked. "What are you going to do to him?" It was the Shaman who answered.

"He shall receive a stronger dose, which will cause him severe amnesia; he will have memory loss covering several years. This memory loss is permanent, hypnosis or other drugs will not work;

his memory is gone and will remain gone." Ham sat in thought. The Grandfather watched him.

"You still want to kill him, don't you?" he asked. Ham looked at the Grandfather while considering his answer.

"Yes, I suppose I do. Maddox is such an evil man and has done so much harm to the creatures; I don't know if I can forgive him. Are you so sure that he will not recover and return here with more men?"

"He will not." Stated the Shaman plainly.

A bone-handled knife fell with a thump in front of Ham, making him jump. He looked up seeking its source.

"My knife, take it." shouted the Grandfather. "He is in that cage over there, blindfolded, gagged and tied. Go! Take the knife, plunge it in with all the force you can muster. Go on! Will that make you feel better? Did you come here to protect the Naha, the bigfoot and the other creatures like you said, or did you come here to satisfy your need for revenge against Maddox?" Ham knew that the Grandfather was right, and he felt ashamed. He had not even admitted the truth to himself. Ham breathed deeply and let out a long breath of air.

"I think, in truth, we both know the answer. His life sign shows that he will live longer. He will not die today. Thank you, Abercrombie, for showing me what I should have known about myself. But you and the Shaman are wrong about that other matter."

The Grandfather laughed aloud. The Shaman pursed her wrinkled lips and shook her head slightly.

"What about us? We know the way here; do you trust us with your secret?"

"Hamish Hamilton, you don't know half our secrets," he laughed. The grandfather turned to his wife and spoke quietly. She got up and left. A few moments later, she returned with a young female bigfoot. She stood a good two meters tall and covered in a pale fawn coloured hair. Her hazel coloured eyes were clear and seemed to show intelligence. The party stared at the Grandfather and then at the bigfoot, and again at the Grandfather as he stood slowly up and took off his buckskins. As he did so, he began to transform, like with Bouchard it seemed just as painful, it was as not quite as noisy, he growled, groaned and roared.

At the same time, the female bigfoot changed; it appeared smoother and less painful process; it was even less noisy. After a few moments, they both stood in front of the group. The female bigfoot had become one of the beautiful maidens who had attended to them earlier; less, of course, her buckskins. The Grandfather had become a larger version of the bigfoot form, bigger, more masculine. He stood proud, his hair streaked with grey, with a grey-white mane crowning his head. Ham sat quiet, hardly breathing.

"Holy shit," was all he whispered. "I never knew."

The maiden smiled at Bouchard, turned and left. Abercrombie changed back, and his wife helped him done his clothes. Ham paused, his face showing deep thoughts.

"You were a Canadian yellow-top bigfoot," he stated to the Grandfather, but also himself.

"Once upon a time, I was a yellow-top, now as you see, I am a grey-top." He chuckled.

"I see what you mean. How come I never knew? Can all bigfoot change?"

"All the bigfoot, stink-apes, yellow-tops etc. that live here can become human if they choose. Why do you think it is so difficult for the bigfoot hunters to find them? Sometimes, members of the hunting parties are bigfoots. Just because we are sometimes creatures, does that mean we are dumb? As for why you don't see that my friend, is your problem. Maybe it is you not Macduff that needs training."

"But we brought the bigfoot, stink-apes and yellow-tops here to the reservation."

"Yes, because they all wanted to come. Remember the sixties and seventies, fast food, fast cars, loud music, Cold War, Vietnam War, drugs, not to mention being hunted in ever decreasing habitat. Look around you; what would you prefer? You didn't bring them, they allowed you to bring them."

"Ok, ok, don't rub it in. What happens to us? You have shown your true selves. Is that not dangerous?"

"I have discussed this matter with Shaman Drygeese and here is what we suggest. We will not drug you this time. Yes, you were drugged the last time, which is why you were having problems finding the entrance. You Hamilton, should return to your home and carry on your work. Bouchard, you may return here any time if you want to live amongst your kind. Yes, we have bear-dogs here as well. Macduff, the Shaman, suggests that you remain here for six months to learn from her. It is a short time, but she says that it will be enough to begin the process of understanding your gift. Janet, go with Ham," and he couldn't resist it, "and be happy." Ham looked at him and groaned inside.

"What about the men outside?" Ham asked.

"They did not see the bigfoot; they did not see the entrance; you will not tell them. Thank them for their service, say that we appreciate them being here for us, they can go with you."

"What do I tell my boss?"

"As little as possible. I think it is understood."

"One last question, the warriors that captured the mercenaries, they were bigfoot? We never saw them, even though we were looking."

"A bigfoot is never seen unless it wants to be. You don't know all our secrets, Hamilton. If a hunter or hiker sees a bigfoot, it is probably leading the person away from something that the bigfoot does not want you to see, like its family, or it is laying a false trail to confuse someone who is getting too close. You will never see a bigfoot's footprint; we fake them very well. Great fun."

Later that day, they emerged from the hidden entrance, minus Macduff. Major and Princess seemed a bit puzzled at this, but a bit of soft talking and stroking seemed to soothe them. The CSOR and SEAL teams did not ask too many questions; it was not their way. They broke camp and started heading for the pickup point close to where they left their parachutes.

Viking Time

It was a late September evening in Largs when the crowd had gone for the day, that Ham took the beasts for their evening walk. To be truthful, Major and Ham walked, Princess, slept in the small rucksack on his back. Ham reached his favourite spot near the boating pond and leaned on the railings. Ham liked the September weather, not too hot and not too cold, just perfect, pity that all the tourists came for the Viking Festival for the first two weeks. Largs had been the location in 1263 when the Scots had defeated the Vikings. Now, this battle was celebrated every September with a fairground and Viking Village. Ham preferred it when it was quiet.

Macduff had been away for about six months, and Ham was looking forward to her return.

The SBS operators were recovering from a troublesome run-in with some evil red-cap dwarves[24] on the Scottish Borders. The matter was solved after the five renegade dwarves, decided that

---

[24] Red Cap Dwarves, so called because they dip their caps in their victim's blood.

living underground away from humans was better than a 50 calibre bullet in the head. It was a strong argument.

Janet helped Ham with an overly playful kelpie which made its home in Loch Ness for a while exciting the tourists at the beginning of the summer tourist season. After they explained to the kelpie the error of its ways and chased it back to the sea, Ham returned to Largs and Janet took some leave and disappeared off to the Shetlands to visit the other side of her family.

Ham was staring out into the darkness. He was wearing his pouch, which gave him some peace. He knew that his wives' ghosts were there, they were always there, but wearing the pouch, he did not have to see or hear them. It was not a matter of love; it was a matter of sanity. Suddenly, he turned, he was startled to find Macduff, smiling, standing right beside him. He had not seen or sensed her until the last minute.

"I see that the Shaman has taught you many tricks," he said.

"Shaman Drygeese taught me many things. I think I will be able to help you more."

"That's good. Did the Shaman also teach you to make a good mug of tea?"

"No, but she did teach me how to make the truth serum."

"Don't you bloody dare!"

Printed in Poland
by Amazon Fulfillment
Poland Sp. z o.o., Wrocław

57441734R00117